Trained for Their Pleasure

A fantasy barbarian romance

Coveted Prey
Book 5

L.V. Lane

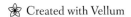 Created with Vellum

Contents

Prologue

Hazel

"Have you ever kissed a boy?" he asks.

"Kissed a boy?" I send a surreptitious glance at the alpha lad sitting beside me on the riverbank. "No, never," I say.

I do not know alphas well, other than the few who pass through Oxenford, our village, which sits on a thoroughfare between north Hydornia and south. My father is a smith and farrier, and his work is held in high regard. Although we are a small village, he gets plenty of work from the local city and those passing through.

"I'm too young to kiss a boy," I say, repeating my father's phrase back to the alpha. I swear, Papa says it twenty times a day and more frequently of late since my body started to change. "I am only thirteen."

I stare at the river. The lad sitting beside me is an alpha, and a little older, although he is not yet a man. He is also so

1

handsome that I think it borders upon beauty. His name is Fen, and I have seen him occasionally when he passes through with his stern older brother.

This is the first time I have really noticed him. And the first time we have spoken.

I'm also sure it is the first time he has noticed me...and my breasts, which he has stared at often in the short time since he arrived. I think he might have stared at them more than the whole of the rest of me. For reasons that elude me, I quite like that he looks at them with an expression somewhere between wonder and pain.

I sneak a glance, finding him staring at the river with a brooding expression. He sends a small branch sailing, and it lands in the river with a splash. A fat toad bounds out of the water, darting straight for us, only to avert course at the last moment.

I squeal.

Fen chuckles. It has a pleasing timbre, although I'm assuredly not happy that he is laughing at my expense.

"It is only a toad," he says.

"I know that," I say, glaring back. I am not scared of a toad like some weak, simpering lass, and I burn with indignation that he is thinking me so. My mother died three years ago, and I have taken responsibility for my younger siblings ever since. My father married again, but she is not a hale woman and is forever supping tonic for some ailment or other. "I was surprised, is all."

Still smirking, he turns toward the river again. I have a strange feeling he does not trust himself to look my way without staring at my breasts. "I would not allow anything to hurt you," he says.

There is a compelling quality to his words. Like he really would not allow anything to hurt me.

Since he is facing away, I allow myself an opportunity to study him. He is twice my size, tall, broad-shouldered and a barbarian, for he comes from the eastern clans. He wears only hide pants and boots, leaving his muscular upper body exposed. My tummy gets a little flutter as I watch his biceps bunch while he pokes about in the grass with another stick. I did not think a man, never mind a lad, could be built thus.

His stick stills, and he turns, catching me in the act of perusing him. Heat flames my cheeks, and my dress becomes tight across my breasts, making the simple act of breathing hard.

"You have hazel eyes," he says. "Is that where you got your name?"

"All babies have blue eyes," I say, feeling like I must be wiser for knowing this fact.

"They are very pretty," he says.

That statement disarms all my thoughts. Now, he is staring at my eyes in a way that makes me breathless once again. I laugh. It is colored with nervousness at being complimented and caught staring at him earlier. "They cannot be that pretty, for you have not looked at them often."

His lips tug up. "I am looking at them now, aren't I?"

"Yes," I agree. "But I think you would rather be looking elsewhere." Happen, we would both rather be looking elsewhere.

His eyes crinkle at the corners with amusement. They are dark brown. I also think them pretty, although they hold an intensity that seems misplaced in one so young.

"You make me wish I had ten sets of eyes so that I could look everywhere at once," he says, smiling. Then his smile drops and the intensity is back. "I want to kiss you. To be the first boy to kiss you. And I don't know why, but looking at your eyes makes me want to kiss you more than when I was looking at your t—"

"Fen! I will tan your fucking hide if you are up to mischief!"

The roar is near enough to rouse the dead. We both start. It is the voice of the stern older alpha. It is the voice of his brother.

"Fuck!" Fen mutters. Smirking, he rolls his eyes. Then he groans, and, capturing my face between his strong hands, plants a swift kiss upon my lips. "I am coming," he hollers back before scrambling to his feet and hastening to his brother's command.

I should go too. I have chores aplenty. Then there are my sibling brats who will be up to all manner of mischief without me there.

But I linger a little longer, for I do not want the spell broken.

My lips tingle. I brush my fingertips over them, imagining Fen's mouth is still there.

When I came to the river, I had never kissed a boy. But now, I have.

I feel both older and yet, too young.

I want to kiss a boy again. But only *that* boy. I want to learn more about the softness of his lips and the tickle of the scruff where his beard is starting to grow. I want to pet all the gleaming muscles. I want to explore all the dips and ridges. I wonder how much stronger such a lad must be compared to me, yet how gentle he was when he cupped my face.

I want to experience things I do not yet understand.

I know kissing leads to rutting. My father is a blunt man who has warned me more times than I can count about lads and their propensity for rutting.

I am too young for rutting. That is for once a lass is married. But I do not think I am too young for kissing.

There is a spring in my step and a lightness in my soul as I return to the cottage. I hope that Fen and his brother have reason to pass through Oxenford often, and that if they do, he might kiss me again.

Only, the Goddess has other plans, and the war with the Blighten sends many men away. I do not see Fen or his brother again. After a while, I cannot even remember the young alpha's face.

Then on my eighteenth birthday, as is expected, I marry a beta male.

Chapter One

Seven years later...

Jack

It has been a good while since I visited the more civilized parts of Hydornia. In the eastern wilderness known as the Hinterlands, my home is a far more barbarous place full of warring clans. I wouldn't have ventured so far from my homelands now had my sister not insisted. She married herself to a fancy lordling a year ago and currently resides in an equally pompous home. With the arrival of a babe, she begged me to visit so that I might meet my nephew.

It has been a miserable year full of conflict, raiding, and other, deeper pain.

Deciding to take a break from my woes, I can admit that I enjoyed myself.

Now, on my return journey, my horse, Sable, pulls a shoe.

There is a bit of damage where it came off, but I know of a good farrier and make a detour to Oxenford.

Unfortunately, this means I won't make it back home today. But better a short delay now than Sable court further damage.

As the king of a barbarian clan, I don't often ride on my own, but on occasion, needs arise where I must. Despite the shitty year, I love my sweet sister and her games to drag me from my melancholic state. It worked, although I'm loath to give the brat credit lest she begin her quest to see me mated again.

And besides, this trip has provided an opportunity for my younger brother, Fen, to step up to his duties toward the clan.

A year to a widower seems like a long time, and yet, no time at all. I'm still an alpha in my prime. I'll take a mate again when I'm ready.

I'm not ready yet.

I miss my mate and the woman she was before her body turned on her. It's not unusual within the clans for a man or woman to take on multiple partners. I know the weak westerners think of us as strange. But even so, it is a practice only done where it's the desire of all involved parties. Lesa tried to encourage me to take a second mate. But I knew it was not a natural inclination in her to share me, nor did I desire another. So, I refused. I'm not the kind of weak alpha to toss a woman aside because she can't carry a child. Our first stillborn took a toll, and no others would catch.

It troubled Lesa.

A lot.

With the death of my parents, she provided a loving influence for my younger sister and brother. I sometimes wonder if her sweetness turned Fen into the troublemaker he is.

I smile to myself as the first cottages of Oxenford come into view. It's true that Fen is nothing but trouble and exhausts me with his antics at times. But he also gave me a distraction when I needed one. And a reason to be.

Sable whinnies. He's impatient and doesn't like being kept to a walk. I pat his neck. "Nearly there, lad."

The high street is a dusty, cobbled affair. A few faces peer at me from doorways, whelps scramble to their mothers, and farming folks tip their heads at me in deference. I'm an alpha and a barbarian, and I look as much.

Ahead is the sign for the farrier, just as I remember it. I wonder if Pike is still running it. The old goat must be close to sixty now. A widower long since. I seem to recall he's had two wives over the years and at least a dozen whelps. When I last saw him, he was well on the path to becoming a crotchety old bastard who enjoys the company of a beer and his buddies, and who is happiest wielding a hammer at his forge.

Each to their own. As the nearest farrier to my homelands, I have called on his services on occasion. He is good with a horse, and his work is of excellent quality.

"Hell and damnation, lass!" The roar comes from the open workshop door. "You've put the fucking forge out!"

Smoke wafts from the entrance. I cannot see the 'lass' responsible for this calamity, but I recognize Pike's voice, and it puts a smile on my face.

"You told me to toss it on!" This voice is feminine and ripe with stress.

"The coal, lass. Not the fucking water!"

"How was I to know which bucket you meant?"

Two muscular arms emerge from the smoke-filled workshop, waving frantically. Their owner, Pike, follows, coughing. Looking about as he finds clear air, he frowns before rushing back into the workshop. He returns, dragging a skinny waif with him, his fist wrapped around her collar.

The lass thrashes about, trying to escape his hold. They are both coughing.

"You'll crack my fucking forge!" he roars, shaking her about.

"I am sorry!" she wails back.

I bite back a laugh, for it's no joking matter if she has tossed a bucket of water onto a hot forge. Yet, I'm drawn toward mirth in a way I've not been in a long while. The sight of the smoke ravaged young woman I fear will imminently receive the disciplining of her life offers joyful entertainment.

Still mounted upon Sable, I clear my throat to gain their attention.

Both heads turn my way. Pike finally stops shaking the lass.

"Jack!" His smoke-grubby face splits into a grin. "You're looking hale. Did you find yourself another mate?" He pauses to frown at the lass whose collar he still grasps in his massive fist. "Go and get some ale an' stew for our guest, lass. An' wash your hands an' face afore you go inside!"

The woman huffs and dares to roll her eyes before stomping off. Dismounting, I tie off the reins.

The last time I passed through here was not long after Lesa's death as I escorted my sister to her new home. Deep into my grieving, I can only imagine the dour facade I must have presented.

"Nay, no mate as yet," I say. "Sable pulled a shoe. I managed to remove it, but it caused a bit of damage."

"Aye, I'll have a look at it," Pike says. "The lass is a nightmare. I'm too old to have brats under my feet." He nudges his head to Sable. "Right foreleg?"

Skimming a broad hand down the leg, he lifts the hoof to inspect. "Not too bad. Do you have the shoe?" Releasing the hoof, he gives Sable another pat as I pull the shoe out of the saddlebag.

"Aye," he says, running his fingers around the rim. "Might be able to reset it, or I can fit a new one if needs be. You staying the night, or do you need me to see to it now? Might take me a while to fire up the forge again. I told the lass to get stew to get her out of my way afore I strangle her. But company's always welcome."

My lips tug up. "Happy to stay and share some stew. How could I refuse? Who is the lass?" I don't want to pry into the man's business, but I'm struggling to assimilate that he's taken a third wife, and such a young one.

"Daughter," he says with a sour expression. "Hazel. By my first wife. Goddess rest her soul—her mother was an angel. Not a bit of her passed on to the brat excepting the way she looks."

He throws a glance over his shoulder. "Hazel! See to our guest's horse," he roars.

The cottage door is flung open, and a slightly less bedraggled version of his daughter emerges.

She is pretty. Blonde hair spilling over shoulders, pert little nose, and cupid bow lips. Small for a beta, but even in the plain pants and shirt, I can see that she has curves.

Hazel. I remember a shy lass peeking at me around her mother's skirts on occasion before her late mother passed away. I also seem to recall Fen getting up to mischief with her by the river when she was still far too young for such things and Fen obsessed with the newness of rutting.

It was not long after our parents died of the pox and a difficult time all around. Fen was forever getting into scrapes. Between his propensity for fighting and the rutting, it was fair to say he turned feral for a while.

The fighting has been tempered a little—he is still obsessed with rutting. Although, I cannot say I blame the lad for urges which are normal for any man and alpha.

I remember white-hot panic assailing me when I realized

the pair of them had snuck off while I'd been busy chatting to Pike. In truth, Fen has never once stepped over the line with an innocent lass. As per my orders, he keeps to the more mature womenfolk of the clan who know what rutting is about and can handle an alpha's rough ways.

Still, as an older brother who has been the responsible adult in his life for many years, I allow that I have at times been overly cautious.

Lost in thought, I realize I have been staring at the lass for too long. Thankfully, she is busy glaring at her father, and he is glaring at her. A sooty smudge marks the tip of her button nose. She looks adorable despite her frown.

I'm surprised when this plainly dressed lass stirs a tightening in my groin. And a little embarrassed for she must be well past an age where a lass is married, and I do not prey upon other men's wives or mates.

"What the fuck are you wearing, lass?" Pike demands, planting broad fists at his hips. "No wonder I can't marry you off when you're always lookin' like a lad. Go an' change into a dress afore you see to the horse."

His words pique my curiosity. A short laugh escapes me as Hazel about faces and stomps off back to the house in a huff.

"Goddess save me," Pike mutters as he heads for a giant barrel and pump before his workshop. Here, he fills a bucket and cleans the worst of the grime from hands, arms, and face. He scrubs himself dry on a rag before motioning me to accompany him into the cottage.

The rough wooden door is swung wide as he enters. It's not intended for an alpha, and I need to dip my head to pass.

Inside, it's darkened with the turn to evening. A single lamp has been lit hanging from a ceiling hook. The grand fireplace is crackling with a blackened pot above, emitting the rich smell of stew. A bedding nook sits to either side of the fire, rough curtains drawn across. It is plainly furnished, with benches to either side of the great table. Dried herbs hang in clumps from the ceiling rafters, adding to the pleasant smell.

Pike waves me toward the table, and we take a seat.

"I thought your whelps were all married," I say, unable to stem my curiosity toward the pretty lass.

"Aye," he says. "Excepting my youngest two lads who are apprenticing with my brother. There are greater needs for weapon skills presently than I possess, and my brother is renowned in the field. It's been a while since I had to deal with a lass afore Hazel returned. Never marry a soldier, I told her. Did she listen? Of course not. He was always off somewhere fighting against the Blighten. No wonder she's not had a brat yet herself. Then he went an' died. She stayed with my sister for a while because I'm too old for this nonsense. Then her uncle went and got handsy with her. I gave the bastard a good beating for it, but alas, my sister begged me not to kill him unless I wanted her and her seven brats on my doorstep seeking food an' shelter. So, he yet lives. Now, I'm lumbered with the whelp again. I should have sent her to my brother and his wife. But it is a week long journey, and Hazel refused to go, claiming that I needed looking after."

Two giant tankards of ale are slammed onto the table between us before his daughter stomps off again.

I find myself smirking—the lass has spirit. Then frowning, for I suffer an irrational urge to visit this handsy uncle and administer a thrashing of my own.

Pike sighs heavily as he lifts the nearest beer to his lips. He drains half of it before he puts it back on the table. "The lass is a test. It's been a year now. I'm seeking a husband for her, afore I strangle her."

"Father!"

Two bowls of stew are deposited with a clatter and thud

that sloshes the contents and nearly spills it onto my lap. I grin at her little tantrum, although my eyes don't linger on the sloshing stew, for I'm captivated by her swaying ass as she flounces off again. No wonder Fen snuck off with her to the river. She is a true beauty with plenty of fire.

"All the finesse of an angry bull," Pike says, shaking his head. "Her late husband took the strap to her bottom, not that it did much good when he was away so often. Some lasses need it daily, or they don't settle into their place. Still, he never complained about the rutting, so there's that."

"I am right here!" she says, dumping a board bearing a loaf and cheese on the table, along with two wooden spoons. "Go on, lass," Pike says, gesturing to me to take the first chunk of bread. "Mind your business when your betters are discussing you. Go an' get us another beer. This talk is thirsty work."

I cough to cover my laugh. When was the last time I laughed? I can't remember, but this unassuming cottage is a bounty of delights.

I cut a thick slice of bread. It's soft in the middle with a nice crusty outside. My mouth waters as I dunk it in the stew. Rich, warming, and full of vegetables and a smattering of meat. Simple and yet tasty—it has been some time since I experienced appetite of any kind.

"Try the cheese," Pike encourages. "The lass is good with the food. Makes it herself. Learned that from her late mother. I shall miss her cheese when she goes."

The lass takes a seat at the table, bowl of stew in hand, and eyes shooting daggers at her father.

I cut a slab of cheese and squeeze it between another slice of bread. I find it sharp and tangy, with a nice creamy texture. Pike is putting his stall out, committed to a somewhat convoluted, yet nevertheless effective, sales pitch.

He nods his head at me, seeing I'm enjoying the food.

"What say you, Jack? A man such as yourself in his prime needs a mate. Don't you have a lad as needs care? She was good with my sister's whelps and with her younger siblings. Her other deficiencies are of small consequence to a man of your mettle who's not afraid to deliver discipline with a belt or strap."

"Father! Must you try to palm me off on every man who passes through?"

"My brother is a man now," I say. For reasons I can't fathom, the previously abhorrent idea of taking another woman has abandoned me. I also don't like the idea of Pike trying to palm Hazel off on every man who passes through. In fact, the thought of someone else claiming all this beauty and fire brings an unexpected twist to my gut. "He does not need so much caring anymore." At least not the kind delivered by a mother...

"Well, that's even better," Pike says, mopping a crust of bread in the gravy at the bottom of his bowl.

"No," Hazel says, dumping her spoon before she has eaten a single mouthful. "You are not going there!"

"What?" Pike says all fake affront. "I'm only mentioning the practicality of bonding to both brothers." He turns to me. "She's twenty summers old, perfect for both of you. Plenty of breeding years left in her."

The lass growls. It is as adorable as the tiny smudge of soot still on her nose.

"I'm not sure I'm inclined toward sharing," I say. This was not a conversation I expected to be having when Sable pulled a shoe. Still, it is a compelling discussion, and despite the lass' vexation, I'm halfway committed, as reckless as that might be.

"Well, that's your choice," Pike says. Picking up his beer, he frowns when he finds it empty. He turns to the lass, who scrapes her chair back as she rises gracelessly to her feet. "I'm only pointing out that should you take her on, it's easier said than done keeping a lusty lad away from a pretty young lass like Hazel. Unless you marry him off. Do you have plans to marry him soon?"

Before I can answer that my brother is an alpha and will mate and not marry, and further, I have needs to temper his ways before I unleash him on any woman for life, Hazel returns with a great jug of ale in her small hands that she dumps on the table. "I do not want a husband, Father. I assuredly do not want two! We have discussed this many times. Do I not wait on you like a servant? Do I not hasten to do your bidding?"

"You try," Pike says. "But you are small and weak for a beta lass, and not practical for anything but the cooking and other womanly things. And besides, what when I die? I'm no youngster. It breaks me to worry about you being left alone."

"I could manage the business," she says, small chin lifting defiantly.

Pike laughs. "Go on, lass. After hauling a few loads of coal, you need to take to the bedding nook for a rest. And the one time you tried to lift the hammer, you dropped it and nearly broke your toe. No, a small weak beta lass like you is much better suited to waiting on a man of means. It's not unusual for brothers to take on the same mate in the clans." He turns to me. "Is your brother an alpha? I never thought to ask."

"He is an alpha," I say, fighting a smile for the lass is spitting mad.

"I'm not an omega," she hisses through clenched teeth. With a huff, she storms off. We both turn as the front door slams in her wake.

I push my empty bowl aside and pick up my beer. "You know she's making a run for it," I say before taking a sip.

"Aye," he shrugs, lips curved in a smile as he reaches for the jug and fills his tankard to the brim. "But she has small legs compared to you. It's only fair she be given a head start."

16

I laugh. "Pike, you are an outrageous father to the poor lass."

"Go on. I'm no such thing. Like to think of myself as being practical. An' I saw you eyeing her ass as she flounced off after nearly dumping stew in your lap. You weren't looking at her unkindly afore, either. The lass has a way that's not for every man. My riling of her was more to test you than the lass. Although I admit, baiting her is fun. I was sorry to hear about your late mate. I respect a man who treats his woman well. A lesser man would have cast her aside. Hazel's husband was a good man but never at home. Whelps, you can't tell 'em a thing."

He drains his tankard while I take all this in. I feel fucking guilty thinking about taking another woman as a mate. But not guilty enough to stop. I doubt my late mate will ever be a subject broached without a measure of pain. Yet, this strange, unexpected moment is *right*.

Pike heaves himself up from the bench. "Despite what the lass says, I've not tried to palm her off on any man afore. It was her aunt who tried that sensing her husband's handsy ways." He nods toward the door. "One of us better get after her afore she gets herself into real trouble."

"I'm not a beta male," I say. "There will be no civilized wedding. We take a woman, and we claim. And my brother—" My brother will want the lass, of that I have no doubt. How I might tolerate his interest, I cannot readily decide. "Is headstrong." Headstrong is putting it mildly. He tests his place with me daily. That he harbors an extreme kind of lust is not unusual in an alpha. That I have forbidden him from fucking any lass' pussy lest we end up with a dozen bastards on our hands is a sore point between us. Our clan's young women are all besotted with him and only too eager to let him use them in all the other ways. "And an extremely dominant male."

I'm not sure why I am stating any of this. My interest in Hazel has taken me by surprise, and it cannot be denied. My reaction should Pike rescind his charity toward me as a man and alpha would not be favorable.

Not since I took Lesa to my furs have I felt this level of possessive compulsion.

My hand shakes a little. "But I do want her," I admit. An alpha is ever a determined beast when he sets his sights upon prey.

"Aye," Pike says, patting my shoulder. "You're a good man and a good alpha. I trust you to ensure your brother does the lass no harm." He lifts his hand. "Now, I've got an inclination toward supping beer with old Pete down the lane. Don't suppose I'll be back until morning."

As the door slams on him, I realize I've not asked him where the fuck the lass might have gone.

Chapter Two

Hazel

I leave home in a huff of indignation and tears. I've no idea where I'm going. I just need to go. I hate my stupid life. I hate my stupid late husband, who was forever off at war and died, leaving me all alone. I hate my father and his plans to marry me off to the warrior alpha who happened upon our home.

I hate my arms that struggle to carry a bag full of coal for my breasts assuredly get in the way.

And I hate my skirts!

"Damn it!" I growl to myself as my dress snags in a branch. "Pox on the stupid dress!" I tug furiously, but it only snags it harder. I have barely made it more than fifty paces before I'm thwarted! Not that I was going anywhere, for it is dark and shadowy in the forest, and I have no desire to fall prey to either bandits or a wolf.

"It is not the dress' fault, lass."

His deep voice brings a flutter to my stomach even as I growl and tug harder on my trapped skirts. The barbaric alpha is built like a bull and a wicked kind of handsome that ties my stupid girl parts in knots.

Both him and his brother, for I have never forgotten my first kiss.

"Oh!"

He crouches at my side, capable hands closing over the hem of my skirt and freeing me with ease. His head lifts, and we both freeze as he studies me in the fading light. His eyes are a stormy blue, and there is a smattering of freckles across his nose. Sensual lips and a rough beard, his face bears compelling masculinity, as does his built, warrior body.

His lips tug up on one side before he rises.

"Goodness." I tilt my chin to take in all of him. As a young girl, I only glimpsed Jack from afar on the occasions when he passed through. His younger brother, Fen, was still a lad when we shared a kiss.

The alpha before me is mature. I have never been in the presence of such a man so closely. He wears naught but hide pants and boots, leaving his broad-shouldered, upper body exposed. A thick leather necklace holds a polished amber stone nestled against the hollow of his throat. Intricate swirling tattoos cover one arm all the way to the wrist. They branch out onto his shoulder. The remainder of his chest and other arm are unadorned. This close, he's impossibly more intimidating. He can't mean to claim me, can he? He's an alpha. I'm only a beta, and a small one at that. Everyone knows omegas are different. That they are better able to take an alpha's cock—I swallow—and their knot.

And even so, he is a barbarian.

"Your father was worried you might get into trouble," he

says, eyes dancing with mirth. "But I see it was only a small amount of trouble—" he gestures toward the ground. "—From a small twig."

My eyes narrow. Now he thinks himself funny! "Do not mention my father and his nefarious plans," I say, planting my fists to my hips. Distantly, I recognize that I'm likely as intimidating as a small angry kitten, but my vexation does not lessen. "And it was assuredly a branch, not a twig!"

He emits a deep guffaw that lights a fire under my growing temper. "A branch," he agrees. "On the small side as might easily be confused with a twig in this poor lighting."

He scoops me up into his arms while I'm still charging my temper. "Come, lass. Let us not linger in the woods. Best I carry you lest another small, twig-like branch assault your skirts."

I am shocked into docility as he stalks back along the shadowy path. I tripped half a dozen times between the entrance to the forest path and the point where my dress got caught—he does not falter once. A cheery glow comes from the cottages as we reach the main street.

"I can walk!" I say, finding my voice again as we exit the forest.

"And I could put you down," he says, making no move to do so. "But I find that I like you where you are."

My chest heaves as delayed awareness courses through my body. His scent is pleasing, spicy, a little earthy, and of the forest. His body is strong and warm against mine. I've heard that alphas emit pheromones that omegas respond to, and yet, I feel tingly simply from finding myself in the arms of such a virile male.

The door to the cottage lays open. He needs to duck to step through. Inside, he lowers me to my feet before turning and pushing the door closed.

I look around, bracing myself for a stern chastisement from my father.

"Where is Papa?" I say. I have not called him Papa since I was a little girl, but I'm feeling small, alone, and vulnerable as it dawns upon me that my father is not here.

"Gone to sup with Pete for the night," Jack says behind me.

My chest stutters. I feel a little faint.

"You mean to bed me, here and now," I say quietly. My mind turns scattered. This cannot be happening.

"I do," he says. I feel the heat as he steps up to me. Not quite touching, but close enough for his rich scent and presence to swamp my thoughts. His hand settles on my shoulder, skimming up, making me shiver as it spans the column of my throat and the upper swell of my breasts.

Goddess, he is so huge and powerful. He will break me for sure.

"I'm a beta," I say like this might douse reason on the moment. Yet, my body responds to his handling. I would be lying to myself if I claimed it was all fear.

"I'm as aware of your status as I'm aware of your body's response to mine," he says. The broad pad of his thumb brushes along the column of my throat, and it turns my insides to a riot of conflicting needs. "Betas can be trained for an alpha's pleasure. It's true; it's not as easy a path as might be expected for an omega. Our pheromones do not hold the same potency. Your body does not weep the copious slick to aid the coupling." His thumb sweeps back down. "Greater skill must be applied to ensure the beta is ready to meet all our needs."

I dare to peek over my shoulder at him. His hot, hooded gaze brings an instant tightening to my belly. I watch his head lower as if it's happening to someone else. His eyes lock with mine. I try to turn away, but his hand holds me perfectly still.

The fingers of his other hand thread through my hair. He grasps it firmly just as his lips enclose mine.

Air traps in my lungs. His gentleness disarms me in a way that brutality never would. I'm sinking under a spell so potent, I wonder if he needs pheromones at all.

His lips are oh so soft as they move over mine before his teeth, nipping gently at my lower lip, encourage me to open. With a small sob of defeat, I part, and his tongue dips lightly inside, tasting me without urgency. It feels entirely natural for my tongue to meet his so that I might also taste. My hands make fists. I am so small before him, my neck stretched up for the kiss, and my hair held like a leash.

There is a slight achy discomfort to the position. My body arches, seeking to give him better access, but he seems in no rush.

His head lifts, and his eyes lower to my lips as he brushes his thumb across them. "What a sweet little beta you are."

I blink a few times. Nostrils flared, I try to find ground. He is an alpha, I remind myself. He is not built like a beta man in any way, but especially not in *that* way. His great strength and size would be enough to contend with, but a beta could never take an alpha's knot.

He releases me and steps back. "You are worrying over nothing," he says like he can read my mind.

I step away, my legs shaky, and glance back when he remains relaxed before the door. "Nothing? Do you not have a cock then? Unless you are a strange kind of alpha, it is assuredly *something*."

He chuckles, and his face lights up in a way that brings a flutter to my chest. "No, lass, that part of me is as alpha as the rest." He steps forward, and I find myself backing toward the table as he stalks closer. He had a presence when he was sitting during supper, but he dominates the small space while standing.

"We are not compatible," I say, although I know of many alphas who have mated to a beta for omegas are very rare. Now I'm wondering how that is possible.

"We don't experience rut as we might with an omega," he says, approaching me with slow but steady steps. "But we can still scent when a beta is fertile, and that can have rut-like effects." He is before me once again. The table is behind me, and I have nowhere to go. "An alpha naturally enjoys fucking."

His blunt words bring a blush to my cheeks.

"But the scent of a fertile beta will rouse an increased appetite, even so. Only unlike a rut, it is far more controlled, but no less compelling need to fill the sweet little beta all up."

Goddess help me; his words are mesmerizing. My pussy grows damp thinking about him filling me all up.

"Of course, it will take the necessary time to train a beta to accept our full needs. Oils can be beneficial, especially in the early stage while stretching a tight little beta pussy out."

"What madness is this?" My eyes are everywhere but on the male before me as I try to block his presence out. I do not want to be stretched! I can't understand why dampness is gathering between my thighs. There must be something wrong with me.

"Do you have some such oil here?" he asks, seeming unperturbed by my outrage. "Or must we do the best we can without?"

"I do not!" I do, in fact, have several oils as might be used in such a way and are natural for the body. "This will not work." My palms land against him to push him away, but the contact is startling. His body dwarfs mine with muscles that are great slabs of hardness under my hands. He leans into me. My fingers clench, petting when I should be pushing him away.

"It will work," he says, voice rough, broad hand claiming mine and pressing it firmer into the hard flesh of his chest. "I have nothing that you cannot be trained to accept. Sometimes, the training is uncomfortable, and sometimes, if the alpha is a bastard, there might be some pain. But I assure you that my cock can and will go all the way into your pussy one way or another. Given enough time and coaxing, the knot will go too. Maybe I will not fill you deeply today. I am both patient and determined. I would rather the experience be closer to uncomfortable than to pain. A little oil will aid that."

His lips lower. He presses kisses to the column of my throat that sets my traitorous body on fire. "Now, my sweet, nervous, little beta, I'm sure your shelves hold something that might be used. But it is your choice. Whether I fuck and claim you, is not. Of course, some betas enjoy a little pain with their pleasure. It is not my place to judge." His teeth nip, bringing a little shiver and a sharp, erotic clench to my pussy. "Is that you, my sweet beta? Do you want it to hurt a little bit as I force my fat dick deep inside you?"

A small groan escapes my clenched lips that brings a hot flush to my cheeks. What kind of deviant creature am I to be aroused by the dreadful image of Jack holding me down and forcing me to accept his monstrous alpha cock into my most delicate place?

I need to clear my throat before I can find words. "I do have something," I say—there is a tremble to my voice.

"Good girl," he says. "Better we build up your tolerance."

Releasing me, he steps back. His scent fills my lungs such that I feel a little dizzy.

I am wet, I realize. Jack has only kissed me and taunted me with his filthy words, and I am wet.

His fingers tip my chin, giving me no choice but to meet his eyes. Then he smiles as his thumb brushes over the tip of my nose.

"A little soot from the mishap with the water," he says with a smirk, then his eyes darken. "Goddess, you are a beautiful, sweet, little thing. I should feel bad about how aroused I am at the thought of ruining your poor little beta cunt. But then again, I am an alpha in every way. Go and get the oil, lass. Then show me which bedding nook is yours."

Chapter Three

Jack

Betas are often confused about the way an alpha can read them. Many female betas presume wrongly that only an omega can satisfy our lust. An omega is naturally more limber, produces copious slick, and is aroused by an alpha's scent. When in heat, they are ravenous for an alpha's touch. You do not need to work hard to drive an omega to sexual highs.

But a sweet, innocent little beta like Hazel will require taming and coaxing before she realizes her full carnal capability. I'm not a green whelp anymore, and I find I enjoy the thought of training Hazel for my pleasure. Where once I might have been impatient, now I am focused on enjoying the journey toward the end game, however long that might take.

The lass is not averse to the idea either. Perhaps she does not realize how sensitive an alpha is to the scent of female lust. Her little pussy is weeping for attention, and I'm only too happy to oblige.

She rummages on the shelf, hands shaking, little ass twitching as she strains to reach the high bottles. I could help her, but I'm enjoying the view. She is small for a beta. I find that appeals to me. It's no secret alphas are predisposed to find an omega form attractive.

Hazel does not have the same enticing scent; this is true. But that leaves me clear-headed for rutting her. Rather than feeling like I'm missing out, I'm enticed by the level of calculation I can apply in making her perfect for me.

Taking a bottle in hand, she lifts the stopper and sniffs before clasping it in her hand. I smirk knowing she has found the one she sought but is fearful of turning around and saying as much. It did not escape my notice how she slipped out a needy groan when I asked if she wanted it to hurt a little as I forced my way deep inside her.

Whether it is merely the thought of pain or the actuality remains to be seen. I hope the latter. Despite me telling her it would only be uncomfortable, there will undoubtedly be some pain before she can fully accommodate all of me.

Still, that cannot be helped. I am invested now. The claiming of her body is a formality, for in my mind, she is already mine. Fen is a lad of limited patience. Better I break the lass in as best I can before she must deal with him.

She is standing still with her back to me, and I see the tension in her shoulders. It is time for me to take control of both the situation and the beta who will soon become my mate.

"Oh!" Her head swings around hearing my approach. The tiny earthen bottle in her hand is fumbled, and I enclose both it and her hand within mine.

"Steady, lass," I say. Extracting it from her shaking hand, I draw her to turn around. "Show me your bedding area."

Her pretty hazel eyes appear luminous in the weak lamplight as I draw my knuckles over her soft cheek.

She nods, hand lifting to indicate the nearby nook. With her small hand in mine, I walk her there before drawing back the curtain. It is cramped, but I will make it work. Once we return to my home, I will rut her in my more spacious bed among the furs.

But I will enjoy this, our first coupling, too.

There are pelts here among the thick woolen blankets, and my cock thickens and lengthens as I take in the details of the space. Omegas are not the only females who enjoy soft things as might be considered a nest of sorts. Hazel's bedding nook is deeply layered. I will get her soft things once home and encourage her to similarly layer my bedding dais to her liking. Her scent saturates it. Soon my scent will saturate it. Alphas are ever basal by nature. The desire to mark both the trembling beta lass and her bedding with my seed is a compulsion that cannot be denied.

I tuck the vial at the edge of the nook and take my sweet beta in hand.

"We don't need all these clothes," I say, closing my fingers over the neck of her dress.

"Goddess!" Her gasp accompanies a tearing sound. I admit to being a little impatient with the clothing, and it might have ripped some under my fingers.

I growl when she tries to interfere. She stills her hands, chest heaving.

"I wish to do the unwrapping," I say, my voice low and barely tempered to be civil. I will go gentle with the lass, but I offer no similar promises toward the clothing that is getting in my fucking way.

The dress drops to the floor. My nostrils flare as I take in the beauty underneath. I catch her wrists together, pinning them at the small of her back when she dares to try and cover herself. My low growl is a warning not to test me. Her scent is enticing. I can smell her pussy weeping for me, and my mouth waters in anticipation of the first taste. With her wrists in one hand, I palm her throat, letting it settle her—letting it settle me.

Her throat is so delicate under my fingers. She is trembling, but her scent tells me it is not all fear.

"Clench your pussy for me," I say.

Her eyes flash to meet mine. "What? Why?"

Releasing her throat, I land a sharp spank to her bottom. "Do not question me, lass. Clench your little pussy and then relax it again."

"Oh," she says. I smirk knowing she has done as she was told.

My open palm presses against the gentle swell of her tummy. "Keep doing it." The way she worries at her lower lip tells me when she clenches. "Does that feel good?" I ask.

I spank her bottom when she doesn't answer.

"Yes!" she says.

Soon, I will push my fingers into her little channel and test how well she grips, but first, I am enrapt by her pretty tits. I cup the weight, bringing a little gasp to her lips. She has full breasts that still look small within my hand. Her nipple buds with this gentle touch, and I swipe my thumb back and forth, watching it bloom under the attention. "You have beautiful fat, nipples, my sweet little beta. Are they sensitive?" I pinch it roughly to test her response.

Her mouth pops open on a little squeak. I pinch and tug harder when she doesn't answer, watching her face contort and flush. "I cannot wait for your tits and belly to grow when you are ripe with child," I say before I can think better about how that might be rushing the lass. Yet the image is both compelling and intensely arousing. The thought of planting my seed in her makes my cock spit pre-cum behind my hide pants. "I think you will make a good little breeder for my brother and me. You will not want for our attention." I am deep into the fantasy now, one I will make into a reality. She is moaning as I pet her nipple, hips rolling in encouragement to rut.

"Do you like the thought of being trained and used for our pleasure?" I ask. "Of being bred?"

"Goddess, yes," she whines.

"Good girl," I say, turning my attention to her other tit, and soon, the little bud is stiff under my rough fingers. "These pretty tits will soon be full with milk for our babes."

My mouth is fucking watering; I have coaxed myself half into a lusty stupor with these words. I am a little rougher than I might be as I lift the lass and drop her onto the bed. She pushes her hair out of her face, lifting to her elbows to watch me. Her lips are parted and swollen from my earlier kiss, and her pretty nipples plump and flushed from my teasing.

As I toe off my boots, her gaze lowers to where my hands work the buckle of my belt. She bites her bottom lip as it drops to the floor. My cock is trapped painfully inside the leg of my hide pants, straining the material obscenely.

I elect not to remove my pants yet. The lass is wary. Getting a look before I have a chance to prepare and fully arouse her to desperation will only traumatize her. Far better I stoke her lust until she is too delirious from pleasure to worry about the claiming.

She falls back as I crawl over her into the nook. Her chest rising and falling unsteadily, a pretty flush to her cheeks and across the upper swell of her breasts. As my hand lowers to cup her cheek, she fills my senses and mind. I want to take her and claim her. I want to feel her pussy enclosing my cock so badly, I fear I may go a little mad.

My hand trembles with the strain of containing my bestial side; I will take this slow if it kills me.

The little minx dares to try and pull away.

My fingers grasp her jaw with a little tempered aggression to remind her that this is not hers to control.

Her eyes flash to meet mine.

"Open your pretty mouth," I growl before lowering my lips to hers. Hazel wriggles underneath me, twisting and pushing against my hold even as her mouth opens and her tongue tangles with mine. She is a mass of conflict. Opening to the kiss and groaning, as she strains to pull away.

My sweet little beta wants to test me, it would seem.

Lifting my head, I shackle her throat with my palm and pin the wriggling little imp to the bed.

My gaze travels down her body, settling on the little nest of dark-blonde curls hiding her pussy from me. When I get her home, it will be my pleasure to shave her so that her treasures are fully exposed. "Open your legs," I command.

With a little huff, she lets her legs fall apart within the limits of my thighs. I push my knees, one at a time, into the gap.

"Goddess!"

My eyes lift to hers before returning to the enticing image of her lush body spread out. Her intimate curls glisten with her juices. I widen my thighs, bringing a little gasp to her lips as it stretches her open. Her bent knees lift as she tries to make space for me.

"What a sweet little beta," I say. "All spread open and vulnerable before her barbarian master."

Her tummy clenches, and she fidgets, small hands fisting over the bedding.

Chapter Four

Hazel

As he leans in, I steel myself for the moment when his lips enclose the stiff peak of my nipple.

"Oh!" He takes just the tip at first, suckling it gently, rough beard tickling and making me squirmy. I want more. I cannot pretend otherwise. Distantly, I know it will hurt when he claims me, but that worry barely impacts the now. Then he opens and sucks half my breast into his hot mouth. My back arches off the bed as the sharp sensation sends sweet nerves flaring to life and dampness pooling between my thighs.

His earthy, male scent surrounds me. His body cages me. The feeling of his mouth tormenting my breast is sublime. It has been so long since I felt a man pleasuring me. Even so, Jack is more than a mere man; he is a barbaric mountain of power and muscle.

He is an alpha.

He lavishes both breasts with attention. Squeezing them together, pinching the nipples, and sucking them a little too hard and yet just right. The alpha fills my awareness. There is no room for other thoughts or considerations when growing arousal fogs my mind to everything but him.

I grow ever more restless. His kisses roam toward my belly then back up over my breasts and throat. He captures my lips in a drugging kiss only to return to my sore breasts. When my wriggling turns frantic, he closes his big hand around my throat and pins me still.

My breath leaves me in a gasp. The sensation of Jack's huge hand holding me is unnerving, yet it makes my pussy clench all at the same time. Words are pouring from my lips in little whiney bits of nonsense.

"Keep still, lass," he growls, head lifting and leveling me with a stern glare. Then his eyes lower, and I know he is looking at my pussy hidden behind my feminine curls. My chest heaves as his hand cups me intimately. I can feel how wet I am there. Goddess save me, I am wanton for his touch and desperate to be filled. "Clench for me," he says as a single thick finger pushes inside.

"Nummmm! Yes! Oh! Please!"

"Best you learn to obey me, lass," he growls. "Or you will get the kind of training when we return to my home that a sweet beta will not enjoy. Bound and pleasured for hours without culmination, and until you better learn your place."

I squeeze, gripping fiercely over his thick finger, and whimpering when all the little nerves inside me zing.

"Goddess test me," he says. "You are so fucking tight." He begins to pump that lone finger in and out. My hips lift, trying to get more of the enticing fullness until he shifts the hand from my throat to pin my hips to the bed. "Bound and pleasured for hours," he says, voice low and menacing. "You will need a great deal of training, I can already tell."

I whimper when he removes his finger, then groan when he

raises it to his lips and sucks it deep into his mouth. The growl he makes is low and rumbly, and I swear I come a little bit.

Nostrils flared, he stares at my pussy, face taking on a determined glint that makes my stomach dip with need.

He shifts, moving out of the bedding nook, making me fearful that he is about to find binding and begin the threatened training now. But instead, he sinks to his knees, pushing my thighs wide to the point of discomfort. Broad hands under my ass, he uses his thumbs to open my pussy, face enrapt by what he has exposed.

Then he lowers his head, and with the first lick, the air is driven from my lungs.

He feasts. There is no other word for the carnality of his sensual assault on my most delicate place. Mouth moving over me, kissing, sucking, licking. He growls lowly when I fret, pinning me more securely within his hands as he continues to eat me out. My mind is spinning. My pussy won't stop clenching, even though there is nothing to clench upon. He is noisy about his business, slurping, growling, and sometimes groaning as he explores every inch of me. His tongue pokes deep into me, thick and sinuous, lapping all around the entrance before lavishing my clit.

I journey into madness under his skilled ministration, straining and panting, begging and groaning.

When he plunges two fingers into my pussy and sucks over my clit, I come in a great heart-pounding, glorious rushing climax.

He laps noisily at my body's offering, but I'm too sensitive, and I grip his hair and try to wrest him away.

His low, rumbling growl makes my stomach tumble over.

"Goddess! Please, stop!"

He does not stop. He takes my small hands in one giant fist and continues to eat me out.

I cannot stand it, everything is over-sensitized, and it courts the cusp of pain. His fingers slam in and out wetly, curving, finding a place deep inside that throbs in a different way. His lips lift from my clit, and instead, his tongue circles the little bud. That is all it takes, and I come once again.

"Fucking delicious," he growls as he lifts his head. Eyes hooded, he inspects my swollen pussy with gentle fingers. "I will need to open you up some more." Reaching for the edge of the bedding, he finds the little bottle of oil. I lie panting as he unstoppers it. A shiver ripples through me when he trickles coldness over my pussy. Thick fingers thrust into me. He pours yet more before working it inside. "Clench and relax for me," he says.

"Oh!"

He uses two fingers. But it's uncomfortable, and more so when I clench. It also feels an achy kind of good. The oil makes me slippery, and the sounds of his fingers fucking into me are wet and squelchy.

"Open your legs wider," he demands.

"I can't!"

Strained as I am around his great bulk, I cannot see how I can give more.

"You can," he says.

A third finger is thrust deep inside me, and I try to jerk away.

His nostrils flare, and his fingers withdraw so quickly, I gasp. The expression on his face is thunderous, and I know I have pushed the beast. I'm flipped over before I can offer a word, and sharp stinging blows are applied to my upturned bottom. "You will learn to obey your lord and master," he says between smacks. "And do so quickly, or you will feel my hand against your naughty bottom."

Goddess help me, he is merciless. I am a jumble of riotous

emotions. Still tingly from my climax, and yet needy, and now suffering the sternest punishment to my bottom I have ever endured. He handles me with ease. There is no escaping the brute. I beg and plead for leniency, but he is a barbaric alpha and relentless.

"You will clench when ordered," he says, applying more spanks to both cheeks.

"You will learn to open your legs and present your pussy for ravishment."

Spank. Spank. Spank.

"You are mine now. I am claiming you. I have already said as much."

Spank. Spank. Spank.

"A lass needs to learn her master's needs."

Spank. Spank. Spank.

"You will learn to present yourself for rutting," he says between more stinging blows.

"On your hands and knees, with your skirt lifted."

Spank. Spank. Spank.

"On your back, with legs spread and pussy on display."

Spank. Spank. Spank.

"Or you may drop to your knees and take my hardened cock into your mouth."

Spank. Spank. Spank.

"I will be sure to let you know if I don't need your pussy or the attention of your mouth. But until I speak, and if I enter the room or look upon you, you should first and foremost assume I need to rut!"

Spank. Spank. Spank.

"If you do not, I shall spank you until I'm satisfied with your repentance. After, I will fuck you roughly to remind you of your place."

My bottom is on fire. My slick pussy is leaking over the

bedding; my face is ravaged by hot tears. I can see now that he will be a stern mate who expects and demands my obedience. "You are a brute!" I say. "And you will not break me!"

The stinging blows cease. I think he might have chuckled. But I'm a mess of snot and tears and throbbing everywhere, and I'm not thinking straight.

"On your knees," he says, tapping my bottom. "Ass up, legs open, and head down. That is how a mate should present."

I'm not yet his mate, but I don't dare to point this out.

I heave myself up, trembling and fearful that he will now finally rut me—the rough edge of his breathing speaks of his great need.

Then he purrs.

I have heard that a purr has a mesmerizing quality to an omega and forces them to be calm. There is no magic trick at work for me, but it is a sweet sound. I understand the sentiments with which he makes it, and that knowledge finds a tender place in the center of my heaving chest. I blink tears back of a different kind as his big hands skim over the surface of my burning bottom.

"That was a firm discipline," he says, voice rough. "Your pretty bottom is inflamed where my hand has been. You are beautiful like this, in your submission to me." His fingers dip between my thighs as he speaks. I tremble with the intensity of the moment. There is pain, but there is also fierce arousal. This alpha has chosen me as his mate, and there is no changing this fact. "Had you behaved for me, I would have taken greater time to prepare you. But I cannot wait anymore."

Tension underlies his words.

I am not the only one trembling, where his fingers pet my pussy, he does the same.

His fingers withdraw.

I swallow. The rustle of clothing being removed is loud in

the dim room. The small lamp is almost out, and soon, it will be dark. I wait. Braced as Jack has instructed, bottom burning and pussy throbbing.

Goddess, I'm so nervous. I talk to myself, lest I do something foolish and try to move.

Then he is with me. His broad hand skimming over the sensitized flesh of my ass brings a hiss to my lips. I bite my lip to hold in my whimpers as the thick, blunt head of his cock slides up and down between my swollen pussy lips.

Grasping my hips firmly as the tip snags my entrance, he pushes slowly inside.

"Goddess!" My inner muscles strain, trying to accommodate his great girth.

He growls, a low warning to be good and still for him. I'm grateful he's holding me tightly enough that I cannot move, lest I anger him again. He begins to thrust, shallow penetrations that tease the entrance to my pussy. I wince as it goes a little deeper. His cock is slick and slippery and enters me with an ease that my straining muscles do not like. I want badly to accept him into my body. There are hints of pleasure to come, although they are overridden by the monstrous strain.

He stops and pulls back so that he snags my entrance. "Fuck yourself onto me," he commands.

Jack

Her head twists around like she is confused by my instruction. The lass has a lot to learn about pleasing me. My eyes narrow as my palm connects with her flushed bottom.

"Oh!"

Her pretty face is as flushed as her ass. She emits a short squeal when I spank her bottom again. The need to claim her is an imperative that cannot be denied. "Fuck yourself back onto my cock," I command, landing a few more lazy but firm spanks when she does not immediately comply. "You are wincing, gasping, and making a lot of fuss when I try to rut you. Now, do as you're told."

My spanking is relentless. I'm deep into my dominance and will broker no dissent.

She tries. The sweet little beta does not enjoy further chastisement to her heated bottom, and she struggles with the task. I keep spanking. But slower, just enough that she does not forget about my command. More wailing and gasping follows, bringing a dark smile to my lips. Her too-tight pussy is both pleasure and pain as she pushes and pulls herself off and on my slippery dick. Her poor pussy clenches at all the wrong times, and she soon grows erratic.

"Good girl," I encourage. "Keep fucking yourself onto my cock. Take it deeper." I back up my command with a series of sharp spanks that see her desperately try to take more. "Gods, you are tight enough to strangle my cock. I will order an appropriate training phallus when we get home." I will make her take it into her tight little pussy whenever I am not rutting her. I grit my teeth in a feral grin as I enjoy her struggles to rut me. I have a feeling she will be naughty about accepting the phallus. I think there will be a great deal of rebellion. I expect I will need to spank her bottom firmly until she is a good girl and accepts it for me.

Despite my determination to let her do this, my hips start to jerk in time with her pushing back.

I rut her with slow enjoyment, spanking her when she dares to falter and forcing her to take more.

"Relax as much as you can," I growl. The poor lass is finally at her limit, her pussy fluttering with the onset of a climax. Soon, she will be perfect for me. Will be opened and able to accept the whole of me. But this straining, quivering tightness is nice too. I thrust harder as she falls limp, finally her exhausted state allowing me to drive deeper until I am at the swollen ridge of my knot. The base of my spine tingles with the need to come. The urge to thrust that little deeper, to force my knot inside her is a near imperative.

I fight it. Reaching around, I find the swollen nub of her clit and strum it without mercy. "Good girl," I say. "Come over your master's cock."

Where these words come from, I cannot say, but it feels right that I am her master. Her body draws tight before her pussy spasms, and a flood gushes over my rod. She throws her head back and squeals as I plunge and hold myself as deep as I dare without knotting the poor lass. My cock spews cum. Great thick jets over and over. My knot is inflamed to the point of pain, and I squeeze it between my fingers, groaning at the intense pleasure. My balls tighten, reaching and straining for the last drops of seed.

Drawing her limp body into my arms, my lips find the juncture of her shoulder and throat, and I bite.

She squeals again, her pussy spasming around me. My grip tightens as I battle the urge to force my knot into her softly clenching sheath.

Gods, she has taken so much this first time. I know I must let her rest; she is yet new to this. But easing my teeth from her throat and my cock from her warmth are my greatest test.

As I pull out, cum spews, and she whimpers. The sound of her pain douses my ardor some. "Hush, love," I say, drawing her into the nook with me and tucking her against my side. My hands cannot be still; they roam over her body as she sobs gently. I need to inspect her. But I'm also an alpha who has claimed a mate. I fear I will rut her again if I do.

The light is out, and the small cottage is filled with shadows. She quietens in my arms. It has been too long since I felt a woman beside me.

I have bitten her.

In the way one might claim an omega.

I have never done that before.

The depth of this urge takes me by surprise as I hold my precious new mate.

Chapter Five

Fen

I cannot see what the fuss is about as Gwen bobs her head over my cock. It is a pleasant feeling, but I do not presume my earthly soul to be exiting my body as a result of her skills.

Not for the first time, I have snuck all the way over to the Halket clan to partake of this lass. Their king's son, Eric, is besotted with her. Given Eric and I are of age and rivals as far back as time, I cannot help but bait him about the lass.

I heard that he gifted her some flowers the other day. What a fucking sap! Gwen is as tall as most beta men and is more skilled with a blade and bow than half of Eric's fucking clan.

I'd sooner cut my dick off than give a lass flowers.

Now is perhaps not the best time to be thinking about cutting off my dick.

Gwen gags a little as I give a particularly enthusiastic thrust. We are in the woods, a short distance from the huts and cottages of her clan. Brandon, my accomplice in this game, is busy rutting her ass. He is not an alpha like me, and I'm irrationally jealous that he can fit his whole cock inside. Although he is a wolf shifter, and even beta shifters have some interesting skills when rutting. As I have learned during the many times we have shared a lass.

"Fuck," Brandon mutters. "She is coming. I need to fucking come."

"Don't fucking come," I growl, although I also want to come. The lass is doing things to my cock with her tongue in her pleasure that are proving to be a test. This will be a poor ruse if we are not caught in the act.

"Too late!" Brandon grunts. "Fuck!"

His hips jerk erratically. He shoves the lass so deeply onto me that I tunnel halfway down her throat. She gags in a way that I do not think is pleasure, and I pull out. I'm not a complete bastard, and I don't want to damage the poor beta lass.

But now I am also coming for her clenching throat before she turned red was absolutely sublime.

She wails in shock as my cum ejects all over her gasping face.

I groan, working myself with my fist until I have spent every drop.

Brandon chuckles as Gwen continues to curse her outrage that I have smothered her in cum.

"We were rutting," I point out as I tuck myself back into my pants. "What did you expect to happen?" I feel a little sleepy now that I have come. Since my mischief has ended in failure, perhaps I can take a nap by the river?

I yawn, and I try not to smile at Gwen's attempts to wipe my copious offering up. All she is doing is spreading it around.

At least this journey was not a complete waste of time...

A sudden roar is all the warning I get before a blur of man charges me. Brandon snatches Gwen out of the way just in time as Eric slams me into a tree.

"Fuck!" I growl. This is the worst possible timing while I am in my post-rutting stupor.

We wrestle. I get a punch in before I'm slammed back into the tree. I see stars until I can shake the daze away. On my periphery, I see the shapes of more people crowding into our small clearing. I hear Brandon shouting. Eric's crew are shouting. Poor Gwen is still bewailing the cum drying in her hair.

For a warrior maiden, she is very prideful about her hair.

"Do not blame Brandon!" I shout and cop a fist to my chin. "Do not blame Gwen either!" I also shout. "The lass is lusty and cannot help herself—uff!" All the air leaves my lungs as Eric slugs me in the gut. His face is nearly as purple as Gwen's when I was choking her on my dick.

Distantly, I recognize now is not the best time to be thinking about lasses choking on my cock.

I get a good uppercut in, and Eric staggers back only to charge me. We both end up grappling on the ground. Here we trade ill-placed blows that wear us out more than deliver actual damage.

Why the fuck was I doing this again?

I grasp Eric in a headlock although I don't think it will hold him for long. Everyone, including Gwen, is now shouting at us to stop. I sense they are trying to wade in and separate us. But our thrashing and kicking is hampering these plans. Eric gets a knee to my balls. It is more of a knee-nudge, but the angle is right, and there is enough pain that I fear I might throw up over him.

"Do not throw up on me!" he growls, tossing me to the side.

We both lie there panting, me clutching my aching balls, Eric clutching his bleeding nose. I will go at him again just as soon as I can get my breath. Our audience wades in, dragging both of us to our feet and putting my plans to an end.

Brandon has planted a hand in the center of my chest. I wave him off.

"Best get yourself a second when you mate the lass," I say to Eric, still a little out of breath. "One cock is definitely not going to be enough."

The crowd surges to try and cut Eric off. But alas, he is powerfully enraged, and the blow sends me sprawling.

Wincing, I test my jaw, eyeing my rival warily. "This was not a fair fight," I say, scowling. "It is well known that only a coward challenges a man who has just rutted a wench."

This time, his crew cut off his charge. There is yet more roaring and cursed threats from my adversary as I stagger to my feet.

Brandon shakes his head at me, but there is a small grin on his lips. I shrug. While I am a little worse for the encounter, it has been a satisfying day. Finally, Eric stabs a finger in my direction and barks at me, "Fuck off my lands."

Pivoting, he snatches up the bedraggled Gwen, who has washed most of my seed off courtesy of an offered water skin. She squeals as he tosses her over his shoulder before stalking off toward their home.

I admit to being impressed that he picked the lass up given she is well built with muscle, and further that, she allowed it.

Brandon bursts out laughing the moment they disappear through the tree. "I have never seen Eric that purple of the face. I think you hit a sore spot telling him she would need a second mate."

I chuckle. "Eric has a powerful right hook. I should not bait him with the lass."

"I don't think you will have the chance to bait him again," Brandon says seriously before his face splits into a grin. "Something tells me his father's plans to bond him to a foreign lass are about to come undone."

I laugh again, and gathering our discarded things, we collect our horses and ride.

Chapter Six

Hazel

An alarming determination that I'm being suffocated rouses me from sleep.

"Mmmmmnh!" My garbled protest is spoken into a wall of hot, hair-roughened flesh. I am on my back, surrounded. Everywhere is more hot skin. I move weakly, finding my legs spread open with a muscular thigh wedged between. My small struggle only wedges the hairy thigh higher, parting my tender pussy lips and catching my swollen clit.

I hiss.

The mountain smothering me shifts, and I suck glorious air into my lungs. A low growl that sets the hairs on the back of my neck rising accompanies a large hand cupping my right breast.

Events of yesterday come rushing back. My pussy clenches, bringing another hiss to my lips.

He squeezes my breast, his growl dipping to that sweet rumbly purr. Head lowering, he sucks my nipple and a good portion of my breast into his mouth.

"Oh! Please!" My fingers grip his hair. I need to gain his attention, but the sensation of his gentle suckling is twisting up my thoughts.

But my bladder is not to be ignored.

"Please, I need to go!" The urgent desire not to embarrass myself by doing my business over my bedding lends strength to my weakened state.

Lifting his head, he levels me with such a stern glare that I nearly empty my aching bladder on the spot.

Then his lips tug up and he shifts off me.

I try to move—I can't. "What has happened to me?" I wail. I have seen day-old kittens with greater vigor. Every inch of me aches but especially between my legs. And my throat; assuredly, I did not expect him to mark me thus.

He chuckles. My anger at him saps the last bit of my energy, and I burst into tears.

"Hush, lass," he says soothingly, scooping me up as I weep in pity at my destroyed body. "I did not mean to make light of your situation." He gains his feet, and with me still in his arms, carries me out the door to where the privy is found. "You are cursed to look adorable whenever you are vexed. And I couldn't help myself."

There are more words of woe on my part as we arrive at the privy. A small verbal battle occurs when he insists that I cannot yet bear my own weight and be left alone. I relent only because my body demands I must *go* now or suffer the consequence. But my face burns the whole time, and I look everywhere but the looming male.

Afterward, when I have finished and can think straight, I realize we are both naked and in plain view of the village's high street!

Jack is without shame in any of this. I am carried back into the house.

I feel shy suddenly as I am placed back in the bedding nook. Last eve's events have fallen under a dream-like haze, but today, it is crystal clear. Still naked, he moves about the little cottage. Even going outside thus and returning with an armful of wood. He tosses wood to the fire, stoking it before putting a pot of water on to heat. I try not to look, but my eyes are drawn to watching the graceful movements of his warrior's body. There are scars scattered among the firm, glorious flesh—large ones and small ones, giving evidence of his brutal life. I have heard about the eastern clans. The people who live there are barbaric and exist in a constant state of war with both the Blighten and themselves.

Soon, this will be my life, too, I realize.

I'm distracted from my rumination by the alpha whose presence dominates the small home. He is industrious, bringing me water to sip, which I take with thanks. This is all curious. I'm not used to being waited on. It's not something one expects an alpha to do.

The heated water is poured into a bowl, and with a woolen cloth in the other hand, he approaches the bedding nook. My eyes grow wider the nearer he comes. The bowl is placed on a nearby shelf.

"What? Oh!" The bedding I had tucked around me is ripped away, and his lusty gaze travels over my body. Turning, he dips the cloth in the water.

I squeak as he plants a hand over my upper arm to keep me still and proceeds to clean me up.

He starts at my face, neck, shoulders, and arms all the way to my fingers. He is careful about it—gentle. I have not been coddled since I was a babe. He cleans every inch of me. I admit, the soft, warmed cloth skimming over my flesh rouses me from my exhaustion and eases the aches at the same time. He lingers on my breasts longer than is warranted for their cleanness. But it feels nice, so I don't complain. His tenderness now is at odds with the rough coupling last night. I feel small and cherished.

My attention is split between shyness given what he does and furtive glances at the rippling muscles of his alpha body. Lulled into a state of relaxation, I'm not prepared when he opens my thighs and applies the hot, dampened cloth to my most intimate place.

Foolishly, I splutter my indignation and receive a sharp slap to my thigh.

"Do not think your weakness will stop me from disciplining you, lass," he says sternly. "I am your mate now. It is my right to see to your care in all ways." He pauses to part the lips of my pussy while my face fills with flames. Crouching, he inspects me with a frown. The cloth is dipped into the water, wrung out, and applied again with his big hand cupping it over my poor, sore pussy. I squirm a little. My skin, dampened from the cloth, springs goose-bumps. My nipples, still tender from last night, harden to pebbles.

The feeling of his hand there makes me clench. Clenching makes me wince. Wincing draws his attention.

He purrs.

Something inside me softens at that deep rumbly sound. It is a beautiful noise, and it makes me think of him as a big growly cat. I am not an omega as might be gentled by the sound. But that he instinctively seeks to soothe me with it brings a tightness to my chest and the spring of tears behind my eyes.

"I wish I were an omega," I whisper.

His face is downcast, eyes on the place where his hand cups me, but he lifts his head suddenly at my words. Dropping the cooled cloth into the bowl, he holds my gaze. "I do not wish that," he says. "If you were an omega, you would be someone else. I do not want someone else."

I blink against the weight forming. His forthright words are plain and yet, beautiful in their sentiments. In truth, I have never desired to be an omega, but in that moment, I wanted only to better please him, and to not be this exhausted burden he must coddle.

But I am pleasing to him anyway.

He does not want someone else.

The spell is broken when he stands. "You are chilled," he says. Gathering a blanket, he wraps me up and lifts me from the bed.

I think I was too busy staring at Jack to pay attention to what he was doing, but there is a cold breakfast laid out on the table with bread, hard cheese, and fruit. Here, he sits with me on his lap.

He holds a small piece of cut apple to my lips.

I blink a few times, concerned with this new development. I eyeball the fruit and him—he is looking very stern, so I don't think defiance or pointing out I have two arms will be in my best interest.

I open my mouth and accept the small offering.

He smiles as I start to chew. It is the kind of smile that lights his stern face, transforming it from one state to another. Then his eyes lower to my lips, and his face darkens. He stares the whole time I am chewing until I swallow nervously. Selecting the next morsel, his eyes lock on my lips.

Goddess, this is awkward. I know many young lasses get to swooning over the thought of being with an alpha. But I never did. All those whispered conversations centered around rutting. Not once did I consider this apparent need to pamper me having ruined my small body.

My late husband was a good man. Although we barely knew one another, he was called away to the war with the

Blighten so often. He was a cheerful man and optimistic despite his years of soldiering. But he never ever fed me!

I am fed. Jack eats only a little.

Wondering where my father is, I glance toward the door. I imagine the embarrassment of him finding me sitting wrapped in a blanket on the stern, naked alpha's lap.

"He is in the workshop, lass," Jack says. "He will not enter until I give permission."

I am shocked by this statement. This is my father's house, yet Papa offers it to Jack with respect because Jack is an alpha. I live in a world rarely touched by the extreme dynamics of alphas and omegas. I have seen alphas pass through as part of patrols on occasion since they are invariably deployed to help in the war against the Blighten. But that is all I know of them. I have never once seen an omega. It is often linked to your parents, or so I have heard. Alphas are more likely to bear alpha children. But there are still the occasional throwbacks that skip many generations only to appear later.

Jack is a dominant male, not only to me, but to all men. Maybe to other alphas, for I sense he is important in ways beyond being an alpha. "What is the name of your clan?" I ask.

"Ralston," he says, pushing the food aside. "It is a prime location on the shore of a loch. There is good fishing and plentiful game. I will provide for you, as a mate should."

I blink as I take in the words and the manner of his speech. There is pride, perhaps a little boastfulness, and danger. A prime location would be highly sought. I do not imagine he got the many scars littering his body through reasons other than conflict.

As his eyes lower to my throat, I suffer an urge to touch the sore place where he bit.

"It will leave a small scar," he says, thumb brushing over the tender skin. The words bring a strange tightening low in my belly. I want to be appalled by his savagery, yet I must admit that such visible evidence of his claiming brings complex emotions clamoring. I am pleased that it is there.

His face is so serious that I could almost forget how he appears when he smiles. Then it softens, and his eyes turn hooded. "Is there anything in one of the jars that might help with the soreness?"

My cheeks heat. Jack is not talking about my throat.

"I will need to rut you again," he says bluntly. Goddess help me. Why does this crude statement make my pussy squeeze and sweet nerves rise?

"There is," I say, voice trembling. Jack is not making idle talk of tomorrow when he says he will rut me. Instinctively, I also know he will not offer me privacy in which to apply it for myself.

He stands, placing a strong arm under my bottom and carrying me like one might do a child. Certainly, our size difference means he suffers no strain. He stops before the high shelving where all the jars are kept.

No sooner do I select a small, stoppered jar than he takes it from me in a way that says he wants no confusion about what will happen next. Taken to the bedding nook, I am laid down. Here, he unwraps me and taps my thigh. "Open your legs nice and wide while I see to the soreness," he says.

I bend my knees and let them fall open, finding riveting interest in the ceiling of my bedding nook. I am a twenty summers old woman. I have been married and widowed. Yet I feel like a young virgin again before this dominant male. We have not yet been properly introduced a full day, and he has already become acquainted with my most intimate places better than any man ought.

Clenching the covers helps me to be still as his fingers gently probe the soreness. The stopper is opened, and soothing oil worked into every part of me. I try desperately not to react. It is impossible. His gentle, intimate inspection and attention is making everything flare to life.

"Oh!" My clit grows sensitive and swollen as he works the oil into it. Pinching it between fingers, he stirs my arousal with ease. Just as my body begins to climb, he shifts, working thick fingers into my channel. I wince and fidget a little. He purrs, although it does not offer much help.

Despite being sore inside after the rough coupling, it soon also begins to feel nice.

"It is a lot for a beta to take," he says, intent upon his task. "But you will gain the capacity to endure once you have been well rutted a few more times."

I'm not convinced I will ever endure his giant rod with ease. This is nice, though. I freely admit that much of what happened last night before he filled my pussy was also pleasurable.

Pleasurable beyond my prior understandings of such things.

I jolt up in the bed when his oil-slicked fingers slide between the cheeks of my ass.

"Goddess! What?!"

"Hush, lass," he says as I blink at him in confused outrage. "You will need to get used to this."

This?

He is exploring all around my little bottom hole with the slicked, blunt tip of his finger. Petting gently over the entrance and making me squirmy such that I cannot possibly be still. It is not unpleasant. It feels a little tingly. I have not thought about being touched there and am confused that it feels a wriggly sort of pleasant.

Then he grabs my thigh in a way that tells me he expects me to struggle and presses the tip of his finger into my bottom.

"Be still," he growls.

My fingers turn white around the bedding—a flush creeps over my face, neck, and across the upper swell of my breasts.

"Please, I don't like it!"

Maintaining eye contact, he continues to do as he pleases. Pressing the tip of his finger in and pulling it out over and over again until I am so confused and conflicted. I must also admit to being deeply aroused. He circles the tightly puckered entrance before breeching me again. This time, he plunges deeper, and I nearly shoot off the bed.

"Goddess save me from this depravity!"

He stops suddenly, brows pulling together in a frown that does not bode well for me. "Your pussy is weeping, lass."

"I—" I have no idea what to say or how to vocalize my outrage and further fear that doing so will provoke my discipline.

"There, lass," he says ominously. "I thought you might need some correction before you could behave and accept this. Lasses who cannot keep still while their masters tend to them get a swift discipline with palm, belt, or strap."

I am turned over, and he sets about delivering heat to my bottom. It is still a little sore from yesterday, and I have no tolerance to endure. Hidden energy surfaces enough to see me struggle and fight in earnest.

He subdues me with ease, spanking my bottom without mercy. It is too much too soon after last night and everything that entailed. I sob piteously even as I curse the alpha out.

My words do not move him. My struggles do not trouble his quest to chastise me severely.

He stops only when he is ready, turning me over. I hiss when my sore bottom is scratched by the rough bedding.

"There, are you yet able to be still?"

I nod, for I do not think I will survive a single spank to my bottom.

My legs are opened. More oil is poured, and he resumes his exploration of my little bottom hole. This time, he does not hesitate to thrust his thick finger in and out. It does not hurt exactly, but it is an unnatural sensation that must be depraved. As he continues to pump and thrust, it soon makes me twitch. I'm sensitive there, both the little entrance and inside, in ways I never suspected.

Soon, I want to come.

Why does this make me want to come?

I am sore, tired, and angry with him for forcing me to accept this. Yet, it stirs latent feelings that make me question whether it is me who is depraved. Perhaps he is similarly confused about my response?

"Stop your fretting," he says. His voice is strained like he is also aroused. Why pushing his finger in and out of my bottom might arouse him, I cannot say. "This is a natural thing for an alpha to enjoy. With training, you will take my cock even here."

I swallow thickly.

"My high appetite for rutting means there will be many times your pussy is sore enough for you to beg me to put it elsewhere. And besides, ass fucking is a delicious kind of tightness. I can see how your pussy is weeping, confused by the pleasure of my attention to your ass. You will take well to this. It is for the best that you do, for I shall have you here either way."

His words unravel me. I am lost.

I come, my ass clenching around his finger, neck arched, and mouth open to offer up the most wanton of moans. It is the darkest of pleasure, earthy, wicked, and he is correct; it is absolutely delicious. His pumping finger slows. Deep inside my bottom, it tickles and tingles.

He drags me to the edge of the bedding nook without warning. His thick rod is lined with my weeping pussy, and he thrusts.

I squeal as sore muscles are forced to give.

"Gods, you are so fucking tight," he growls as he thrusts deep. "It will take weeks of constant rutting to loosen this pussy up."

Yesterday, I did not fully understand what it meant to be with an alpha. To my once innocent mind, I imagined it would be the same as a beta but with a larger cock and a greater appetite. Now, I realize that an alpha has needs that might be considered to be depraved. But if they are, then I am his match.

His mouth crashes over mine as I am still trying to find ground. Hot lips and clashing tongues, I groan into his mouth. The soreness slides from my attention, overwritten by the pleasure of his silken rod as it slams wetly in and out.

My bottom still tingles. I want to come again.

Like he reads my mind, his thick thumb finds my clit and circles it.

He is too rough, but I'm climbing, and it doesn't seem to matter. My climax slams into me with his next thrust, taking me over into the heavenly contractions that try to crush his thrusting rod. He does not stop his pounding. Leaving off my swollen clit, he takes my waist in broad hands and slams me on and off his cock.

I am like a leaf caught in the pull of a rushing river. I am subject to forces beyond my control. Jack will take me how he needs. He will take my ass and my pussy, and although he has only spoken of it as yet, I know he will soon take my mouth.

"Grip me!" he commands.

I do as he says, and the pleasure intensifies once again.

How can I want to come again? How can I be rising amid this rough coupling that should by rights leave me trembling in fear?

He is not asking for my permission. He is taking what is his.

I moan wildly as I feel the thick ridge of his knot bumping against my pussy entrance with every thrust.

"Good girl," he encourages. "My sweet little beta, you were meant to take this. I can feel your hot little cunt fluttering. Come for me. Milk your master of his seed."

I am his to command. He is my master. I sense this in my very soul.

I come, harder and wilder than I have ever done before.

With a roar, he comes with me, flooding me with his seed.

Chapter Seven

Jack

I think I have broken the sweet little beta in my enthusiasm, for she is limp and insentient in the aftermath of the rough rutting.

She whimpers as I ease out of her warmth and a gush of cum spews out. Gods, her poor little pussy is all puffy from my attention. I stare at the mess I have made, feeling my dick jerk in hopeful anticipation of more. My fingers turn white around her slim thighs as I give myself a stern talking to. The poor lass needs some time before I take her again.

We also need to be on our way and return to my home.

I still want to fucking rut her. It is like a year of abstinence is beating down upon me.

Her thighs tremble under my rough handling, and I force myself to let go. What a treasure I have found in this most unexpected of places. The Goddess is indeed mysterious, bringing Hazel into my life.

I brush the hair from her hot cheeks and press a kiss to her forehead. I do not trust myself to kiss her anywhere else given my basal side is riding me hard. Her lashes flutter open as I lift my lips. Her pretty eyes search mine; she seems so innocent, and yet I sense she is corruptible and will come to be perfect for all my rough needs.

And Fen's needs. Although it vexes me that the whelp will get to put his hands upon her, I would need to either leave my home or send Fen away to avoid his interest. He is not ready to lead the clan, and I am not prepared to relinquish my claim. I sigh heavily.

Fen has the capacity for rutting that has been the talk of our clan and every neighboring clan from the day he came of age. I will need to beat the cocky bastard half to death in the hopes of tempering it some before I let him take a turn.

"We need to be leaving soon," I say.

There is the slightest wince on her face. The poor lass is sore, so the journey, even taken slowly, will not be easy for her.

"My younger brother has been left too long alone as it is. The lad has a propensity for trouble that needs to be kept in check. We will travel slowly, but I need to return today."

She nods.

I rise, retrieving my pants and forcing my stiff length inside while having words with it. Alas, there is no hope. I am doomed to travel the entire way with an iron-hard cock and half-formed knot.

I help her to clean up again and to dress. She is pale but only moving with a touch of stiffness and the occasional grimace. There is a small bit of complaining when I tell her there will be no underthings. Sensing my determination in this matter, she does as she is told. The climate is much warmer in the valley that our clan calls home, and she will soon be dressed in the hide dresses that will make her available for my ravishment and pleasure. I smirk, thinking about the protests that are sure to accompany me presenting her with new clothes. I anticipate a great deal of discipline in her future. The lass does try to be good, but she is naturally a brat and needs correction.

Her father returns as we are ready to leave. Despite all his gruff protests that he wished to marry her off, the old goat has tears in his eyes as he gives the lass a hug. Gathering her few personal possessions, I ready Sable. Now that this is done, I am impatient to be home.

I lift Hazel into the saddle before mounting behind her. Her little hiss brings an unwitting smile to my lips, for her discomfort is no laughing matter. But alas, she is cursed to be adorable, and it is hard to keep the grin off my face.

With a wave to old Pike, we ride down Oxenford high street to a gaggle of onlookers. Doubtless, they will soon be gossiping about Pike's poor whelp being absconded in broad daylight by the barbarian king.

We do not travel far before I feel her small body soften against me. She is tired, and that is my fault, I know.

"Once home, you will have leave to rest," I say.

She nods but remains quiet, and I think my sweet little beta is napping.

I was, of course, lying about her having a rest. For I already know that I will be deepening the bonding process by rutting her every chance I get.

Hazel

I spend a good deal of the journey trying to sleep. It is not so easy, and I believe I'm making myself feel worse rather than better. We soon cross the great Yalmore River, taking a steady descent toward his homelands. I have never ventured across the river before, and I admit to experiencing nerves. The trees change notably the further we descend. Becoming taller, with great vines hanging heavily from their branches. They form a canopy around us, bracing the path we follow and sheltering us from the sun.

The air grows humid and warm.

I am still sore, although the oil has helped some. But I'm tired, and when I fail to sleep, I grow fidgety and restless.

"We will stop for a short break," he announces. Urging the horse from the path, he follows a smaller track for a short distance before stopping at the side of a stream. Here, he helps me down.

While he fills the water skins and allows the horse to drink, I go and do my business before cleaning the stickiness that lingers in the stream. He leaves me to it. Goddess, this is all very awkward. Underlying all of this are my fears for the new home and people I am yet to meet.

I wonder about the people of his clan and what they are like.

I wonder about his younger brother, who Jack has said is rough in his ways. I sensed none of this when I last saw Fen, but a good number of years have passed. I dare say we have both changed.

A stick of jerky is passed to me when I return to where Jack waits with the horse. I chew on it while he heads back to the river to fill another water skin. With his proud bearing and a warrior's body, he is no stranger to conflict; the scars tell me as much. But a man of a clan is not only a warrior. He must be a hunter and a farmer even, maybe some of both. The lord over-seeing my former village is a fair-minded man, and we are lucky to be under his guardianship, for not all lords are kind. Will Jack's lord be a fair man? Or will he be a tyrant? My stomach roils as I worry about this, and I put the half-eaten jerky aside. Jack seemed eager to return. If his lord was a monster, I cannot see this would be so. Perhaps it is worry about his brother that drives his determination to return today—he has suggested as much.

He returns to the horse, water skin in hand, walking toward his horse, when he abruptly stops.

He is not looking at the horse; he is looking at me.

Looking at me in the way of a man who wants his mate.

I suck a sharp breath in. He wants to rut me. Right here and right now. I suffer a sudden and foolish urge to run. My pussy clenches. This is what he talked about when he claimed me. Jack wants me, and I'm expected to present. I can see the stillness in him. My chest saws unsteadily as I come to terms with what he needs me to do.

I turn slowly, peeking back at him over my shoulder so that I might better judge his mood. His nostrils flare, and he tosses the water skin aside. Goddess, he really wants me now—wants me to present myself for rutting. My legs turn to jelly as I sink to my knees. My pussy grows wet in anticipation of the dark stretching I will suffer as he forces his monstrous rod inside my tight beta pussy. Bracing my palms to the rough forest floor, I reach one hand back to tug up my skirts.

This is so shameful, presenting myself to a dominant male. I feel so conflicted doing this. My pussy clenches fiercely as the cool air meets the dampness between my legs.

"Good girl," he praises, and my chest swells that I have pleased him. "Cant your ass and entice your mate to rut you."

I swallow. Lowering my head, I widen my thighs and push my ass up. His low growl speaks of great need. I know he is staring at what I have exposed.

"Now, reach your hands back, and pull yourself open so that I can better see where you need my cock."

The alpha's debauchery knows no bounds. Hands shaking, I press my forehead to the floor and pull my bottom open, exposing my feminine place completely to his view.

I hear the clink of his buckle and thud as his belt drops to the floor. Then heat as he kneels behind me. "What a sweet little beta," he rumbles. "Presenting her pussy for a ravishment." The blunt tip of his cock swipes the length of my slit, and I nearly collapse. His low growl warns me to hold the position. "I can see how wet you are from our last coupling. All slick and ready for me to work my cock deeper this time." I hear the pop as he uncorks the bottle of oil he tucked in his pocket earlier. A low groan follows. The sticky sounds tell me he is working oil over his shaft.

Then the tip is presented to my weeping entrance. It slips in a small distance with ease, forcing me to stretch around that bulbous head.

"Goddess, your pussy is a fucking test," he growls. "Lower your hands now, lass, and brace yourself for a rutting."

No sooner do my hands lower when he surges deeply. I gasp, biting my lip against the sudden sting of straining muscles.

"Fucking perfect," he growls. "So fucking tight and slippery." He makes a series of shallow thrusts that have me gasping and fighting the urge to wriggle away from the burning flesh spearing me. "Does it hurt?" he asks as he slowly fucks in and out.

"Yes," I gasp. "It's too big."

"Clench," he demands, following the command up with a sharp spank to my ass. "Good girl. Grip your master's cock and encourage him to fill your pussy with his seed."

"Oh!" I do not like clenching. It makes me ache inside as he thrusts.

"That's my sweet little beta. Now, relax for your master that he might better open you up for his pleasure."

I squeal as he sinks deeper than he has ever before, but he has my hips in a bruising grip and continues to rut me without mercy. My pussy gives under his savagery, and I feel myself take more and more. The sensitive inner walls straining and blooming between fierce pleasure and pain. "I do this for your own benefit," he says. "My brother is not a patient lad, and he will be trying to force his full length and knot into you the moment my back is turned. He is a rough lad with a great appetite for rutting. Once he sees your sweetness, he will not want to slake his lust on any other lass. You must warrant him the same respect you give me. If he needs you, as he will frequently, you will present yourself for his use and ravishment. If your little pussy is too sore, you should take his cock in your mouth and encourage him to spill his seed that way."

Every word is accompanied by him driving a little deeper. I can feel myself opening in ways that alarm me. I try to clench instinctively that it might hope to push the punishing rod out.

He growls. "What a sweet treasure you are, encouraging your alpha to rut you rougher."

I think I'm going numb under this deep rutting, for I cannot feel a thing. As if sensing this, his fingers find my clit, and the sensations come rushing back.

"No!" I wail. I do not want to come. Coming will make me clench over him, and it is the darkest, most depraved climax around an alpha's cock.

"Come for me," he commands. "Come all over my cock. Grip me and encourage me to give you my seed."

I squeal as I come. The dark, skittering pleasure is intense, and my muscles grip so tightly, he can barely force his length in and out. His fingers bite into my hips, and I groan as he thrusts deep.

A climax tears through me, darker and deeper, and I twitch and thrash, all while impaled on him. Body convulsing in dark rapture, I strain to press back in a confused state that impossibly demands more.

He growls, holding me still despite my wild thrashing.

Then I feel it, the thick swelling trying to breach my entrance. Goddess help me. I am not ready for his knot!

"My tummy hurts," I whine. My pussy still clenches around him, and my hips are moving of their own volition as I seek more.

He chuckles. "Naughty lass," he says affectionately. "You are all full up with my cum, yet greedy for more. I will not give you my knot yet. Try and stop milking me, lass, or it might encourage me to force the knot in fully formed."

I clench harder, and it tips me straight into another savage climax.

Jack

She strains, thrashes, and finally falls completely limp on my cock. I ease out of her hot cunt and turn her over gently to make sure she is all right. A weak moan accompanies her stomach clenching, and a great river of cum is ejected from her battered little pussy. "Oh!" Her hips begin to move, lifting and undulating against the ground.

I chuckle. The lass is not suffering; she is merely coming even in her post rutting daze.

Pressing my palm to her flat tummy, I hold her still. Immediately, her pussy clenches and another flood gushes out.

Poor lass, I have really filled her up. I use my finger and thumb to pull her little pussy open, so I can better see how well she has softened. My cock grows stone hard as I watch her try to force my seed out as she continues to come.

My cock jerks, heavy and hot. I want to fill her again.

Tempering my desire, I coax the lass up. She wants to go and clean. I forbid it. Once we arrive at Ralston, I will be burning this fucking dress. "I need to rut you again," I say roughly. "But I can yet wait until we arrive, knowing you are full and scented with my seed."

She swallows and nods, sensing rightly that she should not push me in this matter unless she wants my palm against her ass. I tell myself that she is not an omega, that my scent and cum smothering her do not arouse and comfort her in the same way. I do not fucking care that she is not an omega. And she will learn to accept my ways, or her bottom will spend a lot of time very sore.

I lift her onto the horse, trying unsuccessfully to get the image of her well chastised bottom from my mind. Then I think about how she came hard while I teased her little bottom hole, and I know I will not be able to wait long before I take her in that way.

Chapter Eight

Hazel

I am sticky and twice as sore as I was this morning, which I thought was bad enough. I cannot get the smell of Jack's cum out of my nose. My dress is surely ruined, and it was not like I was allowed to bring more. Every little movement pushes out wetness. Given we are riding, it feels like I am leaking all the time. No one explained that alphas come so much. This is assuredly not an average amount.

But I am drained, and exhaustion pulls me into a fitful doze.

The light has faded toward dusk when he nudges me awake. We skirt the shore of a great loch, and it glistens with magic under the setting sun. Tall trees surround the far shore, but the valley is divided into farming plots on this side. To the center lies the many homes. They sprawl out toward the shore-line and nestle into the lower slopes of the mountain.

My eyes widen in wonder. I have never been in the eastern lands, never mind seen a clan. I had thought them to be basic and brutish because that is how their people appear, but it is nothing of the kind. The homes are all wooden and range in size from modest homes, similar to my father's cottage, to much grander structures twice as high. The design is foreign to me, yet I see the craftsmanship in the ornate gables on the more lavish homes.

As we near, people call greetings. I feel small and shy sitting as I do before this proud warrior. Their attire is strange to me, hide tunics and pants that are sometimes plain and sometimes stained into shades of blue and red.

We pull up outside the grandest building of all. A set of wooden steps lead to double doors. Clearly, it is the home of the clan lord.

Not a lord, I tell myself, for the clans all have kings. My eyes widen as I take in the animal carvings that sweep to either side of the great double doors. The carvings twist and twirl, like they are alive. I cannot wait for daylight so that I might see the wonder well. Upon leaving my father's cottage, I had thought of myself coming to live in rural poverty, but now I see it is nothing of the sort.

I glance over my shoulder at Jack to find him studying me with an expression that is hard to read in the fading light. Has he come to present me to their king?

"What if your king does not like me?" I ask before I can think better about it, for I am nervous suddenly. "What if he makes you send me away?" I did not want this man yesterday. I am still fearful of all the things he intends to do, and there is yet his brother to contend with. But I do not want to be sent away from this alpha who is gentle with me even as he forces me to take his cock. There are good men, and there are wicked men. He may wish to do wickedness to me, but he is not a wicked man, and I want to stay with him very much.

We are mated now, I remind myself, but I am still worried.

"Hail, Jack," a man calls in greeting, distracting us both. He is a warrior, dressed similarly to Jack with broad shoulders and a muscular chest. One arm bears similar tattoos to those on Jack's arm, but they are neither as intricate nor as extensive. "You have returned with a prize!"

Jack laughs as he dismounts the horse before lifting me down.

"Not a prize, a mate," he corrects the man. "Glen, meet Hazel."

Glen bows touching his fingers to his forehead. They are unexpectedly formal here. Rising, Glen calls over his shoulder, and a young lad comes running to collect the horse. A few people gather on the periphery. Some of them hasten up the stairs to open the huge doors. One disappears inside with a tray bearing food and drink.

I try to gawk at the grand house in fear of the king's imminent arrival.

"Where's Fen?" Jack asks the other man.

My tummy gets a little fluttery thinking about Fen. Frowning, Jack draws me against his side. I like having his arm around me, and the way he offers a low purr in seeking to ease my nerves.

"He left a few days ago," Glen says. "Reckoned he was going hunting, but he took Brandon with him, and they did not take only hunting bows. But otherwise, it has been trouble-free in your absence."

"Damn whelp," Jack mutters before tightening his arm around me. "The lass needs rest. We will speak on the morrow."

The man tips his head in deference again and takes his leave.

"Come, lass," Jack says, his eyes darkening as he studies me.

"I promised myself I would let you rest, but I will need you again before we sleep."

I swallow as he takes my hand in his and leads me up the steps. The people waiting at the doors close them around us, leaving us seemingly alone.

A long wooden table dominates, and in the center rests the tray of food and drink. A well-stocked hearth is currently unlit. Several lamps provide illumination.

I am thinking about his determination that he will rut me again. But I am also thinking about the fact that we are in this lordly residence alone.

As I glance up, our eyes meet. I am confused for many stretched moments as I try to dismiss the presented facts.

"This is a grand home," I whisper. "As might belong to a king."

"Aye," he says. "It is all that and mine."

He is not only a warrior. No, Jack is the king and leader of this barbarian clan.

Beyond the main hall is a sectioned-off bedding chamber the size of my father's home. It is dominated by a large, raised platform that is deeply layered with furs and pelts. While the space is enormous, it is also intimate—the bed is inviting. We are alone. I am his now, and there is no turning back. I do not want to turn back, truth be told, but I am nervous all over again.

He undresses me slowly, stripping shoes and layers a piece at a time.

"You will not wear these again," he says, tossing them aside as though disgusted. "You will dress as my mate should when needs be. But you should expect to spend much of your time naked, awaiting my pleasure."

My pussy clenches at this news. I may be Jack's mate, but I

am also lowly. He has told me many times that he will rut me often and intends for me to be gotten with child swiftly. I admit that I have longed to be with a child. My mother died when I was ten. My father married again, but she was not a motherly woman toward any of my father's many whelps. I cared for my younger brothers and sisters until I married myself. Children are a source of noise, conflict, and screaming half the time. But they can also be sweet and find wonder in the simplest of things. It saddened me that I never caught with my late husband, although I take comfort that the Goddess had other plans for me now.

Leaning down, he brushes my long hair over my shoulder before pressing a kiss to the exposed skin. "You are not yet scenting of being fertile," he says. "When was the last time you bled?"

"A few days ago," I say.

He nods, and lifting me into his arms, carries me the small distance to his bed. It is soft underneath me, and the alpha who looms over me is large and dominating.

He is also a king.

I am not ready for any of this. But I do not have a choice.

Rising, he strips his clothes before joining me among the furs. He purrs, and I swear he has already trained me to respond to that sound. Instantly, I am restless, and needy, although I'm still achy inside.

He takes his time. This is not a fierce coupling like I experienced at the riverside. Kisses are long and lingering. They sweep me along into a sensual abyss. I fall into him lovingly and joyously. Every touch is measured to rouse my sensitive flesh. My nipples grow taut under the soft, rhythmic tugging of his lips. My pussy grows slick as his skilled fingers tease my clit.

He explores all of me, drawing me with drugging ease toward climax over and over again.

By the time he rolls above me, I am eager for the welcoming stretch.

There is only a little discomfort this time, and tears trickle over my cheeks, for it is so sinfully sweet.

My knees lift to make a cradle for his hips as he begins to rut me. Even this is gentle, the easing in and out no more than a tease that soon drives me to seek more. My lips find the firm flesh of his biceps, shoulders, and chest. I nip at his strong throat and scrape nails over his broad back.

He will not be rushed nor urged. The more I plead, the more determined he becomes to make me wait.

My aggression rises in proportion to his steady calm.

"My sweet beta kitten has claws," he growls softly beside my ear, and it makes everything clench inside.

Taking my wrists within his hands, he pins them to the furs beside my head, and lifting, begins to rut me with greater vigor. My body is yet newly awakened to an alpha, but it sings under his skilled tutelage.

"Please," I say. "Please, I want your knot."

He growls at this request, fucking into me harder, yet still not giving me the knot. I can feel the enticing roughness pressing against my opening with every thrust. I meet his eyes boldly. It makes all the sensations rippling through me twice as intense.

"You are not ready for my knot, lass," he growls through gritted teeth. "I will knot you when I'm ready and not a moment before. Now, be a good girl and clench over your master's cock that I might fill this needy pussy all up."

I do, and at the same time, he puts his arm under me, canting my ass.

"Goddess!"

His grin is full of wickedness as he finds that perfect angle that makes my pussy quiver. He pounds into me, crushing me against the soft pelt bedding, and I fracture into the heavenly waves. Face contorting with pleasure, he jerks his hips, and I feel the hot flood inside. He growls, easing his hand between us, and I know he is massaging the knot.

I want to do it. I want to be the one who makes his movements erratic and his cock spew cum.

He keeps pumping, more and more, and my tummy begins to ache. I try to wriggle, but he pins me more securely and continues to jerk his hips. Goddess help me, I don't think he will ever stop.

There is too much cum. It leaks out around his hot rod, trickling between my ass cheeks and soaking the bed. He growls, jetting more into me, and my poor tummy cramps with the pressure. "Please, it's too much!"

"I think someone is asking for their first taste of the strap," he growls ominously.

I can feel the thick swelling of his knot pressing at the entrance to my pussy. He stares down at me in the darkened room, I cannot see much of his features, but I *sense* his intent.

He wants to knot me.

I want him to, but I'm also terrified.

He rolls, taking me over him while his cock is still buried deep. My small squeak of protests is met by his growl.

"Be still," he says, grinding me onto his still hard length. He plants a kiss on the top of my head and begins the soothing purr. "Go to sleep, my sweet little beta. I will wake you when I need to rut you again."

Chapter Nine

Fen

"What do you think they are up to?" Brandon asks.

We are in the forest, lying in the undergrowth, watching a four-man group of warriors from the Lyon clan stalking something through the trees. A fat buck lays beside us, which will make a fine meal when we return home. Taking it back will also offer a pretense that we were hunting. Not that I had anything to do with it since Brandon is twice the hunter I am. We have a few shifter families in the clan being so close to the mountains. Mostly, they are like regular families, albeit they can take wolf form. It is always betas. An alpha wolf would never tolerate such a life.

"I do not know," I say. "But it cannot be good. These are Halket lands."

"We are also on Halket lands," Brandon points out with a grin. We have a treaty with them. But I do not believe they are best pleased with me after the incident with Eric and Gwen.

Still, what I should and should not do has never held great sway.

Jack is always complaining that I need to stop these games. But why should I?

The pox is a cruel disease that sweeps through communities from time to time. My mother, who tended to the sick, caught it herself. Then my father would let no other tend to my mother but him. I think he always knew the pox would take her, and he wanted to go with her.

Well, that was fucking selfish of him.

Jack was still a lad no more than fifteen summers old. He fought and killed three alphas who had once been my father's supporters before he could claim his rightful place. It was a vicious, joyless time. The Goddess abandoned me that day. I have not felt her presence since.

Other than that one time when I met that sweet beta lass at Oxenford. I can't even remember her face now, but I remember how she made me feel. An alpha is predisposed to find the smaller, sweeter lasses appealing. It is in our nature to latch, and when we do, it can be hard to break. Hazel was her name. I remember how it matched her pretty eyes.

I sigh. Many years have passed. She has probably wedded and pushed out a few brats by now.

"Do you want me to take a closer look?" Brandon asks.

"No, not yet," I say, squinting. "Also, your wolf hates the Lyon clan. More likely he will savage the fuckers."

Brandon chuckles. He knows this is true. There is a long-standing altercation between him and a Lyon warrior over a certain lass.

Lasses are nothing but trouble whether you mate them or not. Then supposing you find a sweet one like Jack did, and then you lose them?

Maybe Eric has not mentioned our minor altercation over the lass he is too stupid to mate?

No, he will run to his father like the whelp he is. Or one of his minions will tell, or Gwen.

I smirk. Gwen will not tell. She is a lusty lass and always eager for rutting. If Eric wants to keep her for himself, he needs to claim her. And as per my suggestion, he should include his betas in the claiming, or she will never be satisfied.

"I heard they snatched a lass a week ago," Brandon says, drawing my frown.

"Snatched from where?" I ask.

"Halket. She was mated before aught could be done. I heard the Halket king is pissed and has threatened to go to war."

I turn my attention back to the four Lyon warriors. An illness swept through their clan a decade ago, killing more females than males. Now they find themselves with too many warriors and not enough lasses to slake their lust. I think this is behind much of their warring of late. Not that I fucking care. They could negotiate for mates. They could offer their warriors to other clans where there are more mates. Or join the Imperium or the Seven Hydornian kings in the war against the Blighten. All of these are honorable options as befits an honorable man. They could even travel to Blighten lands where they keep young beta women as slaves and free them.

I'm sure once the poor women have gotten over the ordeal, they will be inclined toward rutting with their saviors.

Or maybe not? What do I know of being a slave? At the very least, rescuing them would be better than poaching lasses from other clans.

A sudden scream rents the air, and the Lyon warriors take off running.

"The fuck is that?" I mutter, scrambling to my feet.

"You know what that is," Brandon says, also scrambling to his feet. "What will you do?"

"Challenge them," I say.

He nods, grins in a way that reminds me he is a wolf, and shifts.

I crash through the thick undergrowth in the direction of the scream. There are no more sounds other than the Warriors giving chase.

There are four of them; two are alphas.

There are two of us, and only I am an alpha. But Brandon is a wolf shifter, and that evens things out.

If this is what I think it is, they are attempting another snatch.

If I interfere in the business of other clans, Jack will be pissed.

If I do not interfere, he will probably also be pissed.

If I die, a great many people will probably be relieved. Except maybe the lass who is about to be snatched.

Another scream turns my blood to ice. It is not the playful scream of a willing lass up to mischief. It is the scream of terror, and it sets my blood pounding with rage.

I race, leaping over fallen branches, ax in hand. I'm ready to fight, although I will start a fucking war if I kill a Lyon warrior.

At my side is the steady drum as Brandon keeps pace.

Another scream, this one cut off. But I am upon them, and I roar as I charge.

I burst out into the path where they have taken the lass down onto the ground. I see immediately the dyed leather dress marks her as Halket, for Lyon favors the natural hide like us. She is struggling.

There are no thoughts in my mind, only rage. I swing my ax at the nearest warrior who has turned at my roar. He dodges the strike, but the tip catches the center of his chest. It cleaves through his tunic and flesh underneath, sending a spray of blood arcing. Brandon crashes into the next man, sending him tumbling before falling in beside me on the path.

The poor lass is bleeding from her mouth and stumbles to her feet. The Lyon warriors draw their weapons as we block their path to the young lass.

"Run home, lass," I say, never taking my eyes off my adversaries. "And do not fucking stop until you are all the way there."

Brandon curls his lips back and issues a growl. Behind, I hear the patter of ragged footsteps as the lass flees.

"These is not your lands, whelp," the nearest warrior snarls.

I do not know his name, but I know that if he tries to follow the young woman, I will cut the bastard down. The man whose chest I glanced with my ax is breathing hard. His right hand is pressed to the wound, while his drawn sword is held in his left hand.

I smirk because I am ready for blood, and it is their choice if it flows.

"You know who I am," I say. I recognize two of the lads, and that they have not yet charged, tells me they also know me. "Best you run on back home before I carve you up."

They want to take me; I can see it in their eyes. But they are wary, for I have a reputation for both recklessness and fearlessness. After my parents died, I stopped believing in the Goddess. When I set my mind to it, I fight fast and dirty.

Then there is Brandon, and they know the beta wolf will naturally follow my lead.

The longer they wait, the calmer I become. The lass has had a good head start now, whatever happens.

I feint an attack, and all four of the worthless bastards turn and flee.

I laugh. I laugh so fucking hard, I can barely stand up.

Thank fuck they do not turn back, for they would kill me with ease. When I can get my mirth under control, I find Brandon shifted to human form and glaring at me.

"You are an idiot," he says. Then his face splits in a grin. "But a fierce idiot. I thought Barry was going to piss himself when you faked an attack."

"Barry? That is the fucker's name?" My laughter dies. None of this is a laughing matter. "There will be war," I say sadly.

"This is the second time," Brandon says. "The first time there was a reasonable doubt when the lass claimed it was her decision. This time there is none. Halket will demand recompense or maybe seek war. And at this time of year, right when the Blighten begin their raids."

I nod. I am known for my recklessness and foolishness, but I am also not stupid. Warring among ourselves benefits only the Blighten. The Lyon leader is a bloodthirsty heathen who goes by the name of Rendal. My brother fucking hates him.

He will hate him more now.

"Happen we should do a bit more scouting to see what else the bastards are up to," I say.

Brandon grins and shrugs. "I have nothing else on."

Chapter Ten

Hazel

It is morning, and I'm alone in the giant fur-covered bed. For the second time in as many days, I feel like I've been broken. My poor body resists all attempts at movement. I convince myself it is not as bad as yesterday, but I think in truth, it might be worse.

I'm thirsty, and I need to go. Muttering complaints about amorous alphas, I rise to a sitting position...Then scream for a clanswoman is sitting cross-legged on the bedding chamber floor. Long dark hair falls over her shoulders. Even sitting, I can see she has a long-legged grace.

I clasp a hand to my chest as my breathing evens out. She is eating an apple and looks bored.

"His scent smothers you," she says, nose wrinkling before taking another bite and munching. "I guess you caught him at the right time. Why else would he claim a weak westerner?"

"Where is Jack?" I ask. I know nothing of this woman, but I decide that I don't like her or her bold determination to enter the bedding chamber while I slept. Perhaps it is the way of these people to enter each other's homes?

No, I do not believe that. I recognize mischief when I see it.

"Gone to sort out Fen's mess," she says, tossing her apple core to the floor. "Fen is missing, by the way. Knowing Fen, he's probably gone to start a war with another clan because a war with one is not enough." She rolls her eyes while I try and still the frantic beat of my heart at the mention of 'war'.

Another war, I amend, because it sounds like Fen has already started one.

I look between the woman and the discarded apple core. The room is neat and clean. A shuttered window allows cracks of sunlight in. A colorful woven rug adorns the rough wood floor. Great chests sit at the bottom of the bed and against the wall to my left. They are both ornately carved and quality craftsmanship.

I stare at the apple pointedly. She does not pick it up.

"He said you would need to go and that I was to take you."

At least she has a reason to be here, although the hostility she is projecting does not bode well. Surely there was someone more pleasant Jack could have picked?

But I do need to go, so I heave myself out of bed on unsteady legs. I glance around, frowning when I cannot see my dress. Jack said something about me not wearing it again. Still, I need to wear something, and I see no alternative here.

"Did he leave me aught to wear?" I ask, although I sense this young woman is not about to become my friend.

"No," she says, managing to inject greater boredom. "We do not always wear clothing. Are you afraid to be seen naked?" She peruses my small body in a way that says it is sadly lacking.

I'm not ashamed of my body, but I do not recall seeing anyone naked last eve when we arrived. I'm not green enough to fall for that trick. Snatching a pelt from the bed, I wrap it around myself.

Smirking, she rises to her feet. She is tall and graceful. I've little doubt she would not look as dreadful as I do after rutting. Oh well, I am new here, best not to cause trouble on my first day. I wish that Jack were here, but if what this nameless woman has said is true, I can see that he must do what he can to avoid a war.

When we exit the bedding chamber, I find a few people busy in the main hall, sitting at the long table. A couple of them are engaged in food preparations, chopping vegetables. Two younger girls are weaving baskets under the direction of an older woman.

I freeze. Momentarily stunned that there are people here when it was so quiet yesterday eve.

All eyes turn my way. None of them speak a word. I clutch my fur pelt to me, feeling awkward. It does not cover a great deal of me, and I wish I'd picked up two.

"I don't have all day," my surly escort says, shaking me from my stupor.

Tugging my fur wrap tighter, I hasten after her.

I have no shoes, a point that becomes apparent the moment I reach the gritty ground outside. But I need to go desperately, so I follow the evil gazelle who is stomping off toward the trees. Do they not have a privy here? I cannot imagine going all the way to the forest every time I need to go.

Glancing up, I see that the sun is high in the sky. Maybe this is why my escort is so uncharitable toward me. Many people are busy with tasks, and they all stop and stare at me. One man who is on a ladder busy repairing a roof drops his hammer in his stupor. The man below curses when it lands on his head.

This is all very strange. I'm all but running to keep up with my willowy escort. I'm sure Jack did not instruct her to walk me naked and shoeless!

As we near the trees, I notice there is a path. My bare feet do not like this path any better, but I am here now, so I march on. Hopefully, when Jack returns, he will explain the way of things in his clan that I do not blunder around thus, but this is all very odd, and it makes me uneasy.

The path opens out at a small pool complete with a waterfall.

On the right of the waterfall is a great shimmering oval that spins and warbles, sparkling blue and golden light.

A portal.

I have never seen a portal before, although I have heard about them. It's said that you can feel the presence of the Goddess close to a portal. Many pilgrims travel from the far corners of the world to pay homage and to pray at such sites.

"Oh!" I shiver, sensing the power in the spinning, wondrous creation. I'm confused that the haughty miss would even bring me to such a place.

"You can go here," she says.

"Here?" I ask because this does not seem like the kind of place where a person would *go*. It looks like a place for praying.

"Yes, here," she says, tapping her foot like she is waiting for me to do the deed. She rolls her eyes. "Fine, I will leave you. Don't get lost on the way back. I do not want the blame!"

She stalks off along the path toward Ralston.

I sigh heavily, feeling shaky and all at odds with everything. The pool looks inviting. Maybe I can stay here for a while? It does not sound like Jack will be back for a while, and I can look forward to more awkwardness when I return and must enter the hall where everybody will stare. My stomach rumbles. I am hungry, grubby, and I smell of Jack's cum. It is crusted to my thighs, and I swear I am sticky everywhere. I should go and clean up, but I am entranced by the portal.

Maybe I can stay here for a little while. What is the worst that could happen?

I go and do my business a distance away before returning and dipping my toes in the water. It is cold, but not too cold. Sitting on the edge of the pool, I prop my back against a big, mossy boulder and splash my feet in the water.

Goddess, it feels nice. It is warmer here than in my father's village, and the water is so good. A little sunlight dapples the area through the trees. My eyes drift closed.

I wonder how I should find myself mated to a king as I lay resting beside a magical pool and portal so far away from my former home. I feel a little sad and homesick. I feel a little lost.

These are the Goddess' plans, I tell myself. Who am I to argue with whatever she has in store?

I cannot.

I think I might have fallen asleep.

A great cry rouses me an indeterminate time later.

Chapter Eleven

Jack

I'm going to kill Fen.

This isn't an idle threat. This time, I really will kill him. Goddess bless our late mother's soul, the lad has ever been a test.

The entire day has been wasted trekking all over the fucking place. Meeting with the king of Halket to calm him the fuck down after Fen and Eric fought over some lass they are both rutting.

They are both too old for this foolishness. Fen does not even like the lass in question. He was stirring the other lad up. I will bloody the damn whelp when I get my hands on him, and he will not have the energy to rut anyone for a week!

It helps some that old Karry, the king of Halket, is similarly inclined toward knocking sense into his son as a result.

If it were only the Halket clan I had to contend with, it would not be so bad. But Fen has also gotten into a skirmish with warriors from the Lyon clan, although the details of this are sketchy. It doesn't help that the Lyon clan is twice our size, having taken over territory a year back. Their leader, Rendal, is a bloodthirsty heathen, and I'd sooner go to war than try to apologize to him.

It is likely we will now go to war. It has been brewing for a while. But I would have preferred its timing be by my determination and not the fucking whelp's.

Fen is still nowhere to be found when I return home with Glen and a dozen of my best warriors. I am tired, grumpy, and ready to kill. My men, ever wary of my moods, offer no comment as we travel.

As the sun dips below the horizon, we arrive at the loch shore and slow our horses to a walk.

At least, I have a mate waiting for me when I return. It has been a lonely year. Not long after Lesa's death, the women of my clan tried to entice me into their beds. The foolish ones anyway. Anyone with sense steered clear of me, especially in the early days.

Men come in many shapes and sizes and a variety of dispositions. Alphas are no different, although we have a tighter band around our nature and disposition. When Lesa died, a part of me died with her. There was no urge to rut, no matter how the lasses of the clan might entice me to show them favor.

The Goddess is ever mysterious. My mindset changed when a blonde lass with a sooty smudge on her nose crashed into my life. In so short a time, she has already filled my world. As soon as I get back to my home, I will order every nosy bastard out, take Hazel to my furs, and bury myself in her cunt. Maybe I will give her the knot she seems intent upon begging me for.

No, I will not allow myself to be tempted down that route. My knot thickens my cock to twice its width, and she will need to take several more inches to see me fully seated. She only thinks she can handle me.

"He smiles!" Glen says sarcastically.

I cut him a glare as if to dispute this. "I was thinking about my new mate," I say. "She's convinced she is ready for my knot. It has yet to be two full days, but her enthusiasm is a delight."

He chuckles, but it dies abruptly. As does my own joyful thoughts of rutting my sweet beta mate.

A crowd has gathered outside my home, and in the center, someone has erected a punishment post. Such is reserved only for the fiercest transgressions where a clan member might be subject to a whipping. Torches have been lit. Instantly, I see they have stirred themselves into a frenzy.

I nudge my horse into a trot. Dismounting at the edge of the gathering, I toss the reins to a nearby lad. "What the fuck is going on here?" I demand.

The noise dies as they notice my arrival and the crowd parts for me.

I swear I lose a piece of my earthly soul as I see what they are about. There, tied to the post, is my sweet little beta covered in mud and whatever else they have tossed at her. She is naked, and I can see welt marks upon her skin. My roar is inhuman, and the crowd shrinks back.

"Your slave desecrated the ancient site," Nola snarls, turning to face me. She holds a willow branch—some or all the welting is down to her. As the daughter of an alpha who was my late father's second, she has often had notions above herself. Her father died defending the clan not long before my father passed, and she and her mother have held respected positions ever since. I know she harbored hopes that I might mate her. Whatever this madness is about, she will be lucky to get through it with her life.

My face must show all my fury, for she tries to make a run.

I grab her by the hair and shake her about. "She is your fucking Queen. She may piss on your doorstep for all I care. Were you in some ways confused about her status to me? I will whip any man or woman who does not offer her due respect." I shake her again, my rage so great there is a danger I might snap her neck. I do not have time to deal with her impudence. Seeing Glen, stony-faced beside me, I toss Nola to him. "See that she is suitably punished. After, any unmated warriors may use her for their pleasure."

I waste no time seeing my orders are followed. I expect them to be and trust Glen to show no mercy. Stalking toward the post where my mate hangs trembling, I take my knife and cut her free. She sobs piteously as I gather her into my arms.

I purr. I know it does no fucking good, but I purr anyway.

"Prepare a bath," I bark at the nearest servant as I carry Hazel inside.

I am shaking as hard as the tiny woman in my arms, so great is my rage. I do not understand the details of what has happened, but I recognize mischief when I see it.

Hazel tries to speak as I sit at the edge of the bed, but it is only incoherent babble.

"Hush, lass," I say, rocking her. I think she is worried about smearing her dirt over me.

The servants bustle about preparing her bath. I feel so much guilt at what has happened. It is a wonder the Goddess has not struck me down. Not yet three days have I known her. Not yet three days in my care, and I have allowed this travesty to happen.

When the bath is ready, I carry her over and gently place her in.

She shivers as I wash her, although the water is hot. I want to ask her what happened, but I don't think she can get the words out, and I trust no one else. Once I have her cleaned up, I use fresh water to rinse her off. Wrapping her in a pelt, I take her to the bed.

"Bring some warmed wine," I call to the nearest scurrying servant who is clearing up the bath. I am still dressed, I want to undress, but I don't want to let Hazel go.

I sigh. This has been a testing day. Thanks to Fen, I now have a war with the Lyon clan. I will skin the whelp when he finally shows up. Only now, Fen and his propensity for causing trouble are the least of my concerns.

A servant returns with the wine, and I hold it to Hazel's lips.

"I can't drink," she stammers. "I will spill it."

"What is a little spill?" I say. "Sip it. It will warm you inside."

It takes many moments before she manages to sip it down, but finally, her shivers slow to a faint tremble. She whines when I rise. "I am only undressing, lass," I say. "We need to be skin to skin."

Quietness falls over my home as I return to the furs, pulling her small body flush to mine.

I purr. "I don't know why I fucking purr," I mutter when she fidgets against me. "I have long known that betas find it annoying."

"Why do you think that?" she asks quietly. "I love it when you purr."

"You do?" My hand strays to her bottom, but it is a comforting touch that has nothing to do with rutting.

"I love your purr because it's part of you. I cannot think why anyone would not cherish such a sound and the sentiments in which you make it."

My hands tighten around her. I want to draw her smaller body into mine so that I might protect her better. She disarms me with her sweetness. I have done nothing but rut her. I have, through negligence, allowed her to suffer gravely at the hands of my people. Yet, she still seeks comfort in my arms and my purr.

"Do you miss your first mate?" she asks. We have never spoken about our pasts before, although we have both been bound.

Is she thinking about her late husband? Thinking that he did a better job of caring for her?

It is not my place to feel jealous of one who has been taken into the Goddess' embrace. Nevertheless, I do.

"Aye, sometimes, I do," I say honestly. "And sometimes, I get a sharp feeling in my chest. I feel guilty that I am still alive. I feel guilty that I have found happiness with you and that you have given me a reason to smile again. I take comfort in knowing Lesa is with the Goddess. In her life, she experienced a great deal of pain. That is over for her now. She was not a bitter woman, not even toward the end when she suffered greatly. She begged me to find another mate and to be happy. She was also not afraid to voice her opinions, and I can well imagine her cursing me for my negligence in allowing harm to come to you."

I feel her press a little closer, spilling her tears over my chest.

"Do you miss your late husband?" I ask.

"I did not know him so well," she says. "But he was a brave man who died protecting our lands in the wars against the Blighten. He was cheerful despite his years as a soldier. Mostly, I am sad that I did not get to know him well. And I was sad I never caught with a babe. Now, I understand the Goddess had other plans. But she loves well those who are noble of deed."

My arm tightens. I am ever an alpha and possessive of this sweet lass I have claimed as a mate. The talk of a babe and her past bonded husband has a predictable effect. I curb my urges. Now is not the fucking time.

She grows restless, pressing little kisses against my chest that gain in urgency. I sense what the lass wants, but I will not fucking rut her after what has just happened.

"Please," she begs, weakening my resolve. "I can't stop thinking about it. Please, make it go away."

My growl is low and steeped with both tenderness and aggression. In so short a time, she has become more precious to me than every man and woman I reign over. My cock thickens and lengthens, wanting nothing more than to serve the sweet little beta demanding its attention.

I am still wrestling with what I *think* is best for her when her small hand closes over my shaft. Weak against her needs, I growl lowly, letting her explore me with her gentle fingers. The furs slip aside as she shifts. I steel myself for control, sensing she needs to be the one who drives this moment.

It is dark inside my bedding chamber, but enough moonlight spills through the shuttered window for me to see her pretty, tear-ravaged face. Her eyes implore me.

I nod. "I am yours, Hazel."

Her lashes lower, making a pretty fan against her cheeks as she studies her prize. Taking it in both hands, she explores me with a gentleness that has me gritting my teeth. "You can hold it firmer, lass," I say. "You will not break me."

She sends a furtive glance my way, and biting her lower lip in concentration, grasps me firmly and begins to stroke. My hands make fists as I temper myself not to interfere. My cock is soon leaking over her small fingers, enthusiastic for her attention.

Then she lowers her head and licks the crown, and I swear I see double.

My groan sees her stop to glance at me. "Someone is being a little tease," I say, not unkindly.

Smiling, she goes back to her work, industrious as she laps up all the sticky pre-cum, working her hands up and down erratically and encouraging me to spill more.

I curse softly as she takes the bulbous head into her mouth and begins to suckle me in time with her stroking. I want to fist her hair and choke her on my cock, but now and today is not the time. "I'm going to come," I warn.

The little imp grips tighter and hollows her cheeks as she takes me deeper into her mouth until I butt up against the back of her throat.

"Fuck!" I mutter gruffly as I hear her choke a little in her enthusiasm. I want to drag her off and force her deeper all at the same time. This is fucking torment of the highest order. "There is going to be a lot," I say. My warning is not having the desired effect because she grips her prize and doubles down, using her tongue to lash the length. The base of my spine tingles, my balls draw painfully tight...

Then bliss as I shoot down her willing throat.

I was not lying about there being a lot. Her lips pop off in shock as I'm still coming, and I nearly drown the poor lass. "Goddess!" she says, still pumping her hands. Enrapt by the thick ropy cum that is gushing over her fingers and my belly.

I want to ask her if she swallowed any or if she spat it out. I smirk because I think she spat it out, and I look forward to teaching her how to swallow. I have barely stopped coming, but the thought of training her to suck my cock to my liking has me hardening once again.

"Oh!" she says, her fingers tentatively exploring the thick ridge of my half-formed knot. "This is not going to fit," she murmurs to herself. I think she has forgotten there is an alpha attached to the pole she is handling.

I am tired and a little sleepy after coming, but I am also hungry for a taste of my sweet little beta. The trauma that unfolded outside our home has been put from her mind for now. But I want to make sure she is thoroughly occupied and in no doubt of her status to me as my mate.

I roll, taking her under me. There is a little gasp, followed by a moan as I part her legs and bury my face in between. This is no tender exploration, nor am I inclined toward stoking her arousal with touches and kisses. I just want to fucking feast on what is mine. Her little pussy has already creamed nicely for me. I think my sweet Hazel has enjoyed sucking her master's cock. Small hands grasp my hair, and her legs spread wide enough for them to tremble with the strain.

"Goddess! Yes, oh, please!" Her begging turns incoherent as I get my finger inside her little pussy and find the rough patch that makes a beta sing.

Gods, I want to rut this hot, gushing little pussy. She is becoming perfect for me and responding to my dominant ways. The squelching noise of her wetness drives me wild. I suck her clit roughly as I work my fingertips over the front wall of her pussy.

"No! Oh! Please, stop." Her determination that I should stop only drives me on. She does not dislike what I do. Quite the contrary, my sweet, dirty little beta is about to squirt. She wriggles harder, I pin her harder, and within moments, she gushes all around my fingers and tongue. "Ohgodohgodohgod!'

The bedding furs are soaked. I smirk my approval as I lap at her sensitive clit until she gets all twitchy. I allow her to tug me away this time. I will give her no such allowances tomorrow.

No sooner do I gather Hazel into my arms than she bursts into tears.

"I was so frightened," she says. It is all I can do not to take up my sword and slay every member of my clan.

It is not all their fault, I rationalize.

I purr for her, and eventually, an exhausted sleep pulls her down.

Tomorrow, I will get to the bottom of what occurred.

Then I will take up my sword.

Chapter Twelve

Hazel

When I awake, it is not my pussy that is the first source of discomfort.

My head is pounding, and my eyes are puffy. Yesterday feels like a bad dream.

I rise slowly in the bed. I'm alone. This brings fear rushing until I hear the low rumble of Jack's voice beyond the screen that separates his bedding chamber.

My hand shakes as I push my ratty hair from my face.

Yesterday, I thought I was going to die. As I stood naked, humiliated, and broken, tied against the post, I faced my end.

It is strange how such times bring the past to the fore. Not while I was at the post, my mind was blank to aught but terror then. But after, as I lay in the safety of Jack's arms, the troubled dreams brought many people from my past.

My mother—how I miss her every day. I was ten summers old when she died in childbirth.

I remember my father's stricken face as the midwife tended to her. My younger siblings cried even though they did not know what was wrong.

I dreamed of the day I met my late husband. I dreamed of the day we married. And I dreamed of the day the soldier captain knocked on the cottage door to tell me he was gone.

Grief, it is a strange acquaintance that once met, never really goes.

Life is full of ups and downs. It is never flat or still.

My head aches.

Not for the first time since I left my father's cottage, I feel very alone.

I wonder what will happen to Nola? I heard Jack order her punishment, but I don't remember much else.

Approaching footsteps draw me from my introspection, and Jack enters the bedding chamber. My breath catches seeing his imposing figure. I don't think I will ever look upon him without wonder that this man is now my mate.

Also, as per usual, he wears only hide pants and boots. Does the alpha never wear any clothes? He is a test to my stupid girl parts that he must parade around half naked!

"How do you feel?" he asks.

I want to say I'm fine. But I believe I do not look fine and lying will make him cross. He is at war, I remember. He probably has better things to worry about than me. "I am fine," I say.

He huffs out a breath, but his stern face softens. He strides for the bed, instilling a fearfulness that makes me want to flee. "Hush, lass," he says, gathering both me and the soft fur pelt up. "You do not look fine. You look like I need to go and whip someone for letting this happen to you."

The conviction with which he speaks is unsettling. He is an alpha, I need to remind myself, and they are very different in ways to a beta.

"Today, I will show you your new home. I will introduce you to your people so that they might not be confused about who you are."

"I didn't—"

He stills the beginnings of babbled words by pressing his lips to mine briefly. My breath catches, for even that gentle touch stirs feelings inside that are hitherto foreign to me. "You did naught wrong," he says, looking at me in a stern way that reminds me, as if I could ever forget, that he is an alpha. The memory of the outraged scream as I lay basking beside the pool is grating on my nerves. The wildness as I was dragged from the site naked and driven with sticks and jeers back to Ralston will haunt my dreams.

I'd tried to speak, only to suffer the sting of the willow until I was silenced once again.

The sun had been high when they found me at the pool.

The sun was sinking when Jack finally returned, and my misery was ended.

My shiver does not go unnoticed. Jack's response is a growl. "She will pay for her crime with her life," he says.

"No, please!" I do not know this man well, but those words make me realize how great the gulf is.

"She wanted to kill you," he points out, hands tightening on me. She had certainly compelled the crowd to do just that.

Death? I have seen too much death in my short life. There was a moment as the sun faded when I expected to join those I once knew at the Goddess' side. "I cannot be the reason that someone dies," I say quietly instead. "The others did not know who I was. You cannot blame them."

He continues to growl, and it sets the hairs on the back of my neck rising.

"Are you at war?" I ask before I can think better about how this reveals that I was snooping.

His growl softens to a purr. "We are," he says. That he says 'we' and not 'I' has a jarring impact on me, reminding me that this is my home now. "But that is not a worry for now. First, we shall break the fast. After, I will show you your home."

I don't want to meet the people here again. They have all seen me naked and shamed. I am sure I shall not like anyone.

My stomach rumbles, stirring a chuckle from my mate.

Lifted from the bed while still enswathed in a pelt, he carries me out to the main hall of his home.

Many people bustle about inside while the double doors are open wide. Beyond, I see and hear the industry of people busy. I bury my face in his chest. But I am given no opportunity to hide since he sits at the head of the table and places me on his lap. A bowing older lady arrives with a child, both bearing a platter of food. A jug and earthen cups are set beside the platter before us on the table. Unlike last time, none of the people present look at me. They are all very pointedly looking else-where as they go about their duties.

Like at my father's cottage, Jack selects a morsel and holds it to my lips that I might eat.

"I can feed myself," I say a little mulishly.

He smirks. "Open," he says, staring at my mouth in a way that makes me breathless. I open. He places the berry inside, watching as I chew contentedly on the succulent fruit, enjoying the sugary taste as it fills my mouth.

There are many people in the room, busy with chores, but Jack's eyes never leave me. He watches me as he feeds me, kissing me between bites, toying with my hair, and running his hands soothingly over my back, ass, and arms. Surrounded by him as I am, the attention unnerves me.

The arrival of the huge alpha he called Glen draws my attention and a growl from Jack. It softens to a purr as I turn back to my mate. He feeds me another bite. Suddenly, I'm feeling a little squirmy and needy for reasons I cannot explain. Jack's nostrils flare. "My mate has needs," he says, not looking at the waiting alpha. "Has Nola been suitably punished?"

Jack tugs the pelt a little exposing my right breast to his gaze.

"Yes, Jack," Glen says. "She has not lacked for willing alphas to see to her punishment. What are your orders for her now?"

Jack cups my breast in his big hand, his eyes locked with mine as if daring me to complain. As he captures the nipple and gives a gentle tug, a needy whimper escapes my tightly sealed lips.

"A slave and a gift to the Halket clan. Make sure the alphas who deliver her, remind her often of her new status."

No sooner does Glen's footsteps retreat than the platter upon the table is swept away. The sound as things crash to the floor is jarring. I am put onto the table in their place, and my legs opened before my mate's lustful gaze. "I will see these curls shaved today," he says, running a thick finger the length of my pussy lips. "I will enjoy being able to see all of this pretty pussy. Now it's time I had my breakfast."

"Goddess! This is unseemly!" I say, trying to wriggle away.

He only smirks, unseating me as he drags me to the edge of the table before lowering his head and feasting. I hear the scraping sounds that suggest someone has come to collect the discarded breakfast things, but I screw my eyes shut and pretend it's not happening. I did not know a man might be so obsessed with this kind of thing. It feels like he is trying to fuck me with his tongue.

When he swipes up to lavish my clit with attention, I bite my lips lest I make a sound.

The smack against my thigh is sharp. My eyes flash open to find Jack staring down the table at me. With a gleam in his eyes, he tugs the fur from my body and tosses it to the floor. "Play with your tits while I enjoy my breakfast," he says.

My breath stutters. I try to ignore the servant sweeping up the mess—it is clear that Jack is neither bothered nor about to stop.

"Do you need to feel the strap?" he warns softly. The gentleness with which he tended me last night is gone. The man before me is an alpha with needs. I will do as he says, or he will use the strap. Face flaming, my hands skim up my body until they cup my breasts. I bite my lip hard when even the light brush of my fingers feels good.

Another smack lands, sharper, and I gasp, shooting a scowl at the demanding male.

"Do not bite your fucking lip. I want to hear you. I want everyone to hear all the sounds my mate makes while her alpha is feasting. Now, pinch your nipples nice and hard."

I am terrified of the strap and yet, deeply aroused. My pussy pulses as I pinch my nipples, and a moan escapes my lips. Then Jack's head lowers, and I am lost. My legs are spread wider and tossed over his shoulders. A position that is vulnerable and offers no means of escape. He licks and kisses me with noisy growls and groans. My hips are soon rolling and humping his face as I try to get more of his wicked tongue.

I come with stuttered garbled nonsense, gasping, riding his face without care.

It is only after, as I lay panting, and he rises over me to spear me with his cock that I remember where I am.

Chapter Thirteen

Jack

I told myself I would be gentle with the lass, but I have already failed.

The room has cleared of people, but I know all are aware of what I do and who I do it with.

And why I do it, for I want no one confused about what Hazel is to me.

It does not help me to find restraint when she takes to the rutting so well. There is not a murmur of discomfort as I plow her with my cock.

There is still my knot for her to take—for her to be trained to take—but this is also fucking nice.

Her tits jiggle as I rut her over the table, bouncing under the force of my thrusts. The few things left on the surface bang and rattle about. My knot aches. It grows worse with every rutting, and I temper the need to bury it in her pussy.

I lift her ankles high so that they rest against my shoulders.

The position holds her open for my ravishment as I slam in and out. "Clench your pussy," I demand.

I pin her legs to me and begin to fuck her hard and fast. Her mouth pops open, and her pussy starts that sweet fisting thing it does, encouraging me to spill my seed. The urge to ram my knot deep and experience those heavenly contractions around my thick swelling is near irresistible. Somehow, I grit my teeth and convince myself this is just enough and spill my load with a deep growl.

"Goddess!" she squeals, wriggling when I let my knot sink against her pussy.

It is just a little test, I tell myself. It is only half-formed without full penetration, although I know should I thrust it inside her, it would soon lock.

"Hush, lass," I say, purring as I rock my hips a little. Even this small amount of stretching feels fucking good. "I will need to begin training you to take my knot later." And her ass—I will also need to start training her ass.

And her mouth. There is much training to be done all around. At this rate, I shall never leave the fucking furs.

As I leave her warmth, a great splat of our combined cum hits the floor.

She makes cute little whining noises and clamps her hand over her pussy like she has a hope of holding it all in. I am not best pleased with the people I rule over presently, so some other fucker can clean it up.

I purr for her as I lift her. I have not purred for anyone since I was a child. It is strange to know that she likes it when my first mate never did.

I steel myself for the pain that comes with Lesa's memory, but it is not as sharp today. We live and die by the Goddess' design. She is as often cruel as she is gracious in her gifts. As I carry my sweet little beta mate back to the bedding chamber, I think upon life and upon loss. Who knows when this joy might be snatched from me? That is no way to live fearing what next, so I focus on what I have and the now.

"I have only just gotten up," she says waspishly, reminding me of an angry little kitten, all fierce and yet not much of a threat. "And I have two legs. They will assuredly cease to function if you insist on carrying me everywhere!"

"No need for whining, lass," I say, grinning. "I do not think being carried twice will cause you great problems." I place her carefully against the soft pelts. "I will need to rut you again later. Best you let me tend to any soreness now."

"I can put it on myself!"

She squeaks as I grasp her ankle, unseating her and opening her pretty thighs in one move. The little stoppered bottle rests on the table beside the bed. She gets a couple of smacks to her bottom when she curses. Seething, she lays still and allows me to check her and add a little oil. Her little pussy is all pink, puffy, and full of my seed. I was not very gentle at the table, but it is her own fault for being so perfect that I cannot resist.

I glance up when I hear a noise that sounds a lot like a moan. Her arm is flung across her eyes, and she is biting her lip. Poor little beta is cursed to enjoy all my attention, even as I try to soothe her with the healing oil. Her pretty tits turn flushed as I work my fingers in nice and deep. I am only being a diligent mate. I am not purposely trying to taunt.

She growls when I stop, bringing a smirk to my lips. "Do you want me to carry on?" I ask. "Do you need me to get you off?"

"No!" Her outrage is both swift and fake.

"Sweet lass. There is no shame in being lusty. I know you have already come twice this morning. But it is my duty to care for you in all ways. Do you need my cock again, or would you prefer my fingers or tongue?"

She snatches up the nearest pelt covering her nakedness.

I growl, taking the pelt in hand and tugging it away. "You do not fucking cover yourself from me!" I say, eyes narrowing. "Did we not cover this yesterday?" I don't know why she is protesting so much. I'm confident that should I leave her alone for a moment, her small fingers will be rubbing her fat little clit until she comes by her own hand.

"I do not need to come," she repeats.

My face softens as I take in the whole of her, including the faint bruising where the switch landed. I trace my finger along the line over her arm before leaning in to brush it with my lips. "Yesterday was not as I would wish. I'm sorry for that. I would like you to rest today. Tomorrow, I will begin training you for my pleasure."

She swallows, and her slim thighs twitch in a way that says she is not averse to my plans.

A polite knock comes to the entrance to the bedding chamber, rousing my attention from my mate. Turning, I find Jessa waiting there. Jessa is a sweet lass with not a bit of spite in her. A much better disposition to care for my mate. She bobs a quick bow. Her hands are laden with a great bundle of pelts and soft things as might make a perfect nest.

"I have the pelts, sire," she says, shooting a swift glance at my mate before lowering her lashes.

.

Chapter Fourteen

Hazel

Jessa is a sweet young woman and nothing like Nola. She helps me into a short tunic dress made of hide before showing me where I can *go*. It is right behind the building, as one might expect. Then she insists that all the pelts she brought should be placed to my liking on Jack's giant bed.

It seems like too many furs for one bed. But she's insistent. She is also nice to me, and I don't want to offend my new friend.

So all the pelts go on until it resembles a giant animal nest.

I secretly admire the deeply layered softness. Who doesn't like to sleep somewhere soft? Jessa assures me this is perfectly acceptable.

I'm doubtful. But it *is* blissful.

I'm tired from the rutting and the stress of yesterday, so I sleep through the afternoon.

Then Jack returns. His purr is absolutely manic when he finds me in the pelt mountain. He puts me on my hands and knees and ruts me so wildly that the thick pelts are tossed all over the place. He seems pleased about the mess he has made. After, he tucks me against him, throwing a heavy leg and arm over me until I can barely breathe.

My panicky wriggling sees him pin me tighter, and closing his teeth over the back of my neck, he bites down. Despite this making no sense, I drift straight into sleep.

We fall into a pattern over the next few days. I explore a little more of this community that is now my home every day. Nola has been sent as a slave gift to a neighboring clan. The beta was not well liked, I soon learn, and other than her mother, who yet lives here, few are sorry she has gone. Those who I meet now are full of deference toward me. I make a few friends among the women and soon have chores I can help with when Jack is not demanding my attention.

I have always enjoyed cooking, and such tasks add a pleasant kind of purpose. Many of the women are with child or have little ones running about. The children are always up to some mischief or other, and I laugh a lot.

But there is an underlying tension for Jack's brother, Fen, still has not returned. Then there is the looming war that is sparking between a neighboring clan and us. There have been a couple of minor skirmishes, but the tension is building, and I worry about what will happen next.

But it is now morning again, and as per routine, Jack feeds me and then feeds *upon* me. Hitherto meeting Jack, I did not know this was a thing that men engaged in. Maybe it is an alpha thing?

Alas, today's feasting is interrupted by the arrival of his second alpha, Glen.

"Your brother has returned," Glen says. Throwing an arm across my eyes, I try not to think about my position of being laid open upon the huge oak table with my mate's head between my thighs. I was very close and want badly to snarl my displeasure at the male who interrupts us, even as flames engulf my cheeks.

Jack growls against my pussy—I think I come a little—before he surges to his feet.

"The whelp can wait," he says. Grasping my wrist, he tugs my arm from over my eyes and pins it to the table while reaching for his belt with the other hand.

He spears me in a single thrust. News of his brother has stoked his aggression, and he ruts me roughly. I think Glen might have left, but I'm too busy enjoying myself. When Jack first rutted me, he would be careful to keep the burgeoning knot outside. Now I feel the little ridge sliding against my pussy entrance with every thrust, and he only holds it outside when it swells as he comes.

His face is an image of stern determination. I gasp and sometimes squeal when he surges too deeply, and the pleasure turns to pain. Big hands grasp my waist as he shuttles in and out.

"Goddess!"

I struggle as he continues to batter against that sensitive spot inside. My nails rake over his arms, but it only drives him on.

"Open your legs," he commands. "Do I need to take the strap to your naughty bottom before you can be good?"

I am like a ragdoll being broken on his cock, but I do not want to feel the strap. The pain is doing strange things to me. My pussy gushes around his rod so that the rutting makes the most obscene, wet sounds.

"Good girl," he purrs. "You are taking this so well. I am almost all the way inside your hot little cunt. I think some time with the strap before this evening's rut will help you to better relax and take all of me." His eyes are locked on the place where he spears me.

Suddenly, he rips his cock from me, and pinning me against the table, strums my clit without mercy.

"Oh!"

"Beg me for my cock," he demands. He pauses the strumming just as I'm about to come and lands a sharp smack against my thigh. He pinches and pets the little pleasure nub before strumming it roughly again.

"Beg your master for his cock. Beg me to get all the way up inside this tight little beta pussy."

He alternates between rough strumming, stinging spanks, and petting my slippery clit until I fear I am about to lose my mind. My hoarse wailing must be heard for miles.

"Please, fill me. Please! I need all of it!"

I come the moment he surges into me. There is some pain, but it acts as a trigger, making my pussy grasp his length harder.

He growls as he holds me pinned to him. Inside, I feel the gush of cum filling me...and the knot swelling. He snarls as he jerks out. Fisting his cock, he works it roughly, covering my pussy and belly with thick white ropes of his seed.

I lay panting.

He nearly knotted me.

He was all the way up inside me. He nearly stretched my poor beta pussy with his knot.

The thought of being knotted no longer fills me with dread. "I need my master's knot," I say on a moan. My hands are on my pussy before I can better think how this might come across. The fingers of one hand spear inside while the others rub roughly over my swollen clit.

"Good girl," he croons. "What a perfect, filthy little beta I have found. Getting herself off on the thought of taking her master's cock and knot."

Wanting to come again, I groan. My fingers do not feel as

good as when Jack does it. All I do is make myself hungrier for more of him.

A sob bursts from my chest. I am tired, but I am also needy in ways I do not understand.

His eyes meet mine, and his nostrils flare. "You are adjusting to being with an alpha," he says, smoothing a hand over my hot cheek. "This is normal, lass. You are naturally lusty. Although you do not scent my pheromones in the way an omega might, they are still acting upon you." He stuffs his still hardened cock into his pants and carries me through to the bedding chamber where he lays me on the bed. "You will take my knot naturally when you are most fertile," he says, eyes hooded as he inspects me. "My brother has returned, and I must deal with him. But first, I need to scent you some more."

His hands lower to his pants, thrusting them down his hips far enough for his fat cock to pop out.

My pussy clenches at the sight.

"Just lie there for me like a good girl," he says, spreading my legs open as he jerks his hand up and down his ruddy cock. "I need to get my seed over you. Then you will take a nap while I deal with Fen."

I am already smeared with his cum. Thick globs of pre-cum leak from the tip. It drips over my pussy, belly, and breasts with every pump of his fist. "You are not to wash this off," he says, voice low, and gaze enrapt by the fresh splattering of his seed covering me. "It is rich with my pheromones, and it will further drive your beta body to respond."

I pant, captivated by the rapture contorting his face. Being covered in his seed, and further, sleeping thus, should horrify me, but my pussy only weeps in anticipation of his marking.

He growls, teeth bared as he shoots load after load of thick cum over me. I gasp in shock as more and more spills and splatters over my body from my pussy all the way to my throat.

I tremble in the aftermath. Taking my small hand, he presses it into the thickest pool of cum, and uses it to spread it around, over my breasts, up to my throat. The scent invades me. I am shaking with equal part shock and arousal. Alphas are a strange yet compellingly basal breed of males.

He smirks, pleased with the mess he has made. "You are well claimed," he says, pride coloring his voice.

A thick pelt is selected and wrapped around me. Then I am told to sleep until he returns.

Despite my determination that I am not sleepy, I do drift into sleep.

Chapter Fifteen

Fen

J ack is going to be pissed. I can sense the mood in the clan as Brandon and myself arrive. Everyone is presuming I have fucked up again. If I have, then for once it was not my intention.

We come to a halt in the small square outside my home where Jack's second, Glen, approaches us.

"It will take more than a buck to improve his mood," Glen says, pointing at the deer carcass resting over my shoulder. It weighs a fucking ton. I let it drop, and it hits the dusty ground with a thud. I do not mention that it is the second buck we caught. The first one was abandoned long since when we caught the Lyon warriors trying to snatch a Halket lass.

"He cannot be in that bad a mood," I say, rubbing a hand through my hair while gesturing toward the open double doors. From inside comes the unmistakable sounds of a lass being pleasured.

Being pleasured very well if her wild moans are anything to go by.

It is not an unpleasant sound. It is entirely pleasing, if I were honest, but it has been a good while since I felt Gwen's clever tongue, and it is having a predictable effect.

"He has broken his abstinence from rutting then?" I venture to ask. It must be my brother. I cannot imagine anyone in the clan bold enough to commandeer his home for rutting a lass.

"A mate," Glen says, smirking.

"Nola?" Brandon asks, copping a scowl from both Glen and me.

"No fucking way would Jack bed Nola," I say...Unless the lass has drugged him. I turn to Glen. "It's not Nola, is it?" I do not like the lass well. She often has ideas above her station. I feel a little sick at the thought of it being Nola.

"It is not fucking Nola," Glen says with surprising vehemence. "It is a western lass he brought back after visiting your sister. Nola has been banished to Halket as a slave for some mischief she engaged in."

"Fuck!" Brandon says inadequately.

Inside, the wails of pleasure rise.

"Aye," Glen says, lips a flat line of displeasure. "I'd not mention her name in Jack's presence. It was only his new mate's insistence that Nola be shown mercy that saved the troublemaker's life."

Mate? I cannot believe Jack has taken on a mate. He showed no inclination toward claiming one before he left. The Goddess plays mysterious games.

The news of Nola's mischief worries me, and I am not sorry she has been banished. Yet, there are other graver concerns at large. I need to talk to Jack and tell him everything I have learned.

"Maybe I should wait," I say.

Glen's lips tug up in a smirk. "He could be in there a while. Maybe the rest of the day. But I know he is keen to learn all about your antics that have left us under the threat of war. I will venture to check his mood."

I nod my thanks, and Glen strides off up the steps.

The groans of pleasure stop, and I swallow. I knew there would be trouble after I chased the warriors off. How the fuck do I find myself in these situations? Here I am outside my own fucking home waiting with my head up my ass while Glen goes in to assess my brother's mood!

Glen returns a short time later, a smirk on his lips as he makes his way down the steps. The sounds of rough rutting, moans, and growls of pleasure can be clearly heard. It is not only the lass taking pleasure now. Thank fuck I cannot see inside from where I stand.

"He said the whelp can fucking wait," Glen says, still grinning. "But I believe he will be done shortly."

He points at the dead buck. Better take that to be dealt with.

Shortly turns out to be fucking ages. The rutting has done little to soften Jack's mood, for he is wearing an expression like thunder when he comes upon me sitting on my ass on the shore of the loch.

Brandon slinks off, leaving me to suffer my brother's wrath alone.

"So you have a mate then," I say, turning back to the glistening water and sending a stone skimming the surface.

"You have started a fucking war! Now is not the time to sit skimming fucking rocks like a fucking whelp!"

I jump to my feet, pissed with his assumption that I am the wrongdoer in this. He is always fast with his fucking assumptions. "It is a pity you are not as fucking fast with your rutting as you are with your fucking blame. Then I would not be out here skimming stones like a fucking whelp!"

His face softens some. "So you have a good reason for causing conflict with Lyon? I had hoped as much. And as for rutting, I am not a green whelp dipping his cock for the first time. Although I admit, the poor lass was sore, and I needed to tend to her. She is yet new to being with an alpha, and there is much training to do."

I swallow hard. I don't yet know this lass he has taken as a mate. Yet that my brother is clearly smitten with both the lass and her pussy, piques my interest. Given his year's abstinence, I cannot begrudge him his newfound joy.

"Lyon warriors were trying to snatch a lass," I say. "We were hunting after the incident with Gwen." I assume Jack has heard about that part. His scowl suggests he has. "I do not think the first lass who found herself suddenly mated went by choice. Seeing four warriors on Halket lands, we followed. They caught a lass. Not so far from the village either. I think they were going to rut her then and there. I bloodied one with my blade. It was enough to give them pause so the lass could run for home. I stood my ground, and the warriors fled like the cowards they are."

"There have been a couple of skirmishes," he says. "You best be fucking sure the lass was not willing if we are about to go to war over it."

"She was not fucking willing," I say, scowling and fighting my temper. "I know the sound of an unwilling lass. She was screaming until they struck her to quieten her down. Had we not been there, she would have been rutted and taken off as one of their mates, maybe all of theirs."

His face softens. He nods and puts a hand on my shoulder. "I was only asking, Fen. I do not willingly go to war. But I fucking hate that bastard they call a leader. I find myself anticipating the joy in carving him up more than is sensible for a man who has recently acquired a mate."

"The timing is not good," I agree. I side-eye Jack, trying to gauge his mood, for I am curious about his mate.

"No," he says, eyes narrowing.

"What?" I say faking affront.

"You will meet the lass when I am fucking ready and not before."

"Is she pretty?"

"I am still pissed about what happened with Gwen," he says.

My smirk grows. "She is pretty," I say. He has all but admitted as much by not disputing it.

"There is more to a lass than being pretty," he says.

I glance his way. "She has big tits and takes well to rutting—uff!" I cannot believe he has fucking cuffed me. "If her wild moans of pleasure after you learned I had arrived are anything to go by," I say, still risking the opportunity to bait. "I think you're worried the lass might prefer me."

His dark gaze is unsettling. It is not unusual for brothers to share a mate. I have never considered such an idea before, although I am no stranger to sharing a lass or enjoying more than one. Outside of the clans, our ways are considered scandalous by some. I cannot imagine any other way.

Still, I always assumed I'd mate more than one lass rather than the other way around.

"How pretty?" I venture to ask.

As he stares at me, I see the tic thumping in his jaw and the stiffening of his posture. I feel like I am standing on shifting ground, and I don't know what any of this means.

"Come, best we meet with our warriors. Then we will need to send word to Halket for this will involve them."

Chapter Sixteen

Hazel

Thirst and hunger rouse me from sleep...and stickiness. I am also sticky such that I need to peel the pelt from my skin. There is always a jug and bowl waiting with a soft woolen towel on the small table before the shuttered window. I pad over and clean myself up.

I now possess several hide dresses that are scandalously short and barely cover my breasts, courtesy of a few easily undone ties. Ties, that I might add, squash my breasts together. Further, the material does not meet fully and places my cleavage on display. I swear the clothing was sent by the Goddess herself to tempt a man toward rutting. It presents everything they might want to touch in an enticing package. There is no underwear, which means my ass and pussy are available for Jack's big hands to pet, pinch, or pat.

Sometimes, he gets a gleam in his eye, and the short skirt is thrust up before he sets about rutting me without a care for where we might be or who is around. It seems to be the way of things around here. A man may be mated or wed to one or more women, just as a woman may be bound to one or more men. I am not the only lass who is absconded for swift rutting without warning. The males all seem to possess a constant and vigorous appetite—it is a wonder anything gets done!

I spend the afternoon helping the clan womenfolk with some food preparation, but as the light fades, I wonder about Jack and his long-absent brother, Fen.

Returning to the home, I find it quiet. Food will be brought at Jack's request, so I pad into the bedding chamber to wash my hands and face.

Low voices rouse me from the task, and I wipe myself off on the waiting woolen towel.

One voice is Jack, but the other is unknown. Curious, I approach the entrance to the bedding chamber and peer out.

I am quiet, but the two men seem to sense me, and both heads swing my way.

I swallow. I know instantly that the man standing beside my mate is Fen, Jack's brother. Jack is always calling him a whelp and further speaks often of Fen's foolishness. In my mind, he was still the young lad I met at the riverbank and with whom I shared my first kiss. I barely recognize this strapping alpha, who, while younger than Jack, is every bit as intimidating. They look similar in features—Fen is not as brawny as his older brother, but Goddess, he is as handsome as sin with his darker hair and eyes. A lazy smirk lights his face as his gaze drinks me in.

He looks hungry. They both look hungry and not in the way of a man needing food.

I blink a few times.

I swallow again.

This is what Jack spoke about. I'm supposed to present to both him and his brother.

Goddess, this is shameful, but I also do not want a punishment with the strap. Jack has threatened to use the strap tonight to prepare me to take all of his cock better. I cannot imagine how much worse it will be for me if I fail my duties now.

Turning around, I peek back over my shoulder to double-check. No, they are both still staring at me like they are barely restraining themselves from falling upon me. I need to do this. I really need to present myself for their ravishment.

My pussy grows damp in anticipation. I see Fen's nostrils flare. Goddess, it is still shocking to consider that an alpha can scent my lust. Drawing a ragged breath in, I sink to my knees, and face flaming, reach back to lift my skirt.

"Fuck," Fen mutters roughly. "I have gone a little light-headed so swiftly has the blood rushed to my cock."

I hear a thud and Fen grunts. I peek back again to see the brothers glaring at one another before both their faces swing my way.

Fen groans as though in great pain. I do not think Jack hit him that hard?

"This is not a rutting time," Jack says harshly. "Go to the bedding chamber, lass, and await me there."

Tears pool in my eyes as embarrassment fills me that I have gotten this wrong. Snatching my skirt down, I flee the room.

Fen

I understood that Jack had taken himself a mate, and further, that she was pretty. The word pretty does not do justice to the Goddess-blessed beauty who just entered the room.

Then she sank to her knees, lifted the hem of her scandalously short dress, and presented herself for ravishment.

My brain stopped functioning as I took in that sight.

145

Then Jack acted like a dick, and the poor lass was sent running from the room.

I can hear her sobbing. It builds my temper to the point where I am ready to knock some sense into my older brother.

"What the fuck was that about?" I demand, glaring at the thick-skinned oaf who has no business being anyone's mate. There is something strangely compelling about the lass who just entered the room. Like I know her. Yet, Glen mentioned she was a westerner, so she is not from a clan. Our sister must have introduced them. Becka was always seeking to find me a mate when she was here. It makes sense that she would be up to the same mischief with Jack, even though he is more surly than I ever was.

I can also see why such a lass would tempt any man to change his views on mating. I have never been inclined toward taking a mate before.

Before. As I embrace this revelation, it shocks me. The entry of the tiny beta into my life is like a blow between the eyes...and other places.

"I told her to fucking present if I looked like I was in need," Jack growls. "I was not expecting her to present the first time she clapped eyes upon you!"

I smirk a little inside, although I am still pissed at his handling of this. Had we rutted the lass—as she clearly needed —she would not be upset now.

He runs a tense hand through his hair like he is thinking about rutting her still. I admit I am thinking about rutting her, too. Gods, the image of her slick little pussy waiting for a cock to plow it is emblazoned upon my mind.

"Hazel has taken well to my needs," he adds, staring in the direction of the bedding chamber.

Hazel, I frown. Why does that name stir at memories? "What the fuck was she wearing?" I ask. "Is that her native dress? It is very short." I have never seen a westerner dressed thus, but perhaps it is an obscure village. A thousand thoughts about the Goddess in human flesh are swirling around my mind, yet it is this one that finds voice. I cannot honestly say that I mind the length of her dress, although I can see me getting into a fight with every fucking alpha in the clan if I catch any of them admiring her plentiful charms.

"I need to rut her often," Jack says by way of explanation, copping a raised brow from me.

"I'm not surprised if she is walking about like that all the time," I say. "Worse still if she is constantly flaunting her pussy. Is it a cultural thing? Where the fuck did you find her?"

He gives me a shifty look. "Oxenford," he says.

"Oxenford?" I repeat like I am one of those talking birds that repeat your words back.

"I ordered the dress to be shortened because I need to rut her often. And she only flaunts her pussy to me because I told her it's what I expect, and further, that I will take the strap to her bottom if she does not. The lass has the worst sense of timing. She has never done it before another male."

I try to unpick that jumble of revelations, but I am still thinking about Oxenford. Only now, my attention has narrowed to a moment by the riverside when I was but a boy. I try to mesh the memory of a pretty young lass over the stunning woman mated to Jack. She has changed. Of that, there is no doubt. Yet those pretty hazel eyes that peeked at me under her lashes at the side of the river are the same ones seeking my approval a moment ago when she presented herself. I groan a little to myself and try to get my raging hard-on under control.

I thought of her often after I boldly stole her first kiss. But as the time went on, her face lost clarity in my memory. Soon, all that remained was the feel of her sweet lips. She was thirteen at the time. I'd presumed the lass to have gotten married and pushed out a couple of brats long since.

"Pike's lass," I say. It is not a question, but Jack nods.

My brother is a year a widower, and he has been a miserable bastard for all of that time. His late mate, Lesa, was a sweet thing, and I understood that it cut him deeply when she joined the Goddess. He was mated to Lesa when I was but a boy. I never thought of her as aught but a motherly figure. But I am no longer a boy, and I do not feel the same way toward the sweet beta Jack has claimed.

For so long, the Goddess has been absent from my life. I felt her all too briefly that day by the river. But now, and today, I sense her once again.

I feel like Hazel was mine first, although many years and distance have kept us apart.

I feel like I want to challenge Jack for rights to her.

I feel like I might go on a rampage if he tries keeping her from me.

"She is very small," I say. I am a rough alpha, although I would never seek to hurt a lass. Jack has forbidden me from taking any but the more mature, hale betas who are well used to rutting. But I am an alpha and predisposed to find interest in the smaller, sweeter ones who better resemble an omega. Hazel is a tiny lass. When I first saw her, I was sure she was an omega until I realized there was no scent.

She is small and sweet, and she fucking presented to me for rutting. She gave me—okay, I stole—her first kiss. I don't care what Jack says. She also met my eyes before she turned and lifted her skirt.

I groan as the image of her peeking back at me brings a rushing roar of blood pounding.

He will need to fucking banish me to stop me from rutting her. I cannot think straight; the need is so sharp and all-consuming. "I do not want to be fucking banished," I say. "I will go on a fucking rampage if you try to keep her from me."

I am slammed up against the wall as the last words leave my lips.

His fist encloses my throat. I may be younger, but we are well-matched, and I could push him off if I chose.

I do not choose to. Her first kiss might have been mine, but Jack has claimed her first. He is the king, as is his right as first-born. I do not begrudge him his place as our leader; I am not well disposed to such a role. But today, I am thinking about challenging him.

"If you talk like an ass and a whelp, you will be treated as one," he growls, face inches from mine, daring me to resist.

"It is not I who set the lass to sobbing," I point out.

He growls and jerks away from me, eyes shifting toward the bedding chamber hidden from our view by a screen.

Also, he has not said he will banish me.

He is thinking about sharing her with me.

"We will share her," I say.

His nostrils flare. He is still glaring, but he nods his head.

"We will share her," he agrees.

Chapter Seventeen

Hazel

I can't stop crying. I don't think I have ever felt rejection as deeply as when Jack ordered me to the bedding chamber. I am angry at him, but I'm also angry at myself.

I also recognize that the only reason I'm so upset is that I have come to crave the alpha, both his intimate attention and his soft purrs. I do not even mind that he feeds me!

Then there is Fen, the lad who claimed my first kiss. For so long, his image was seared into my mind, but then time happened, and all I remember is the way my tummy tumbled over when he smiled. I have been wedded and lost a husband during the intervening years. Young girl's dreams of stolen kisses have no place in the adult world.

Yet here he is.

Here we all are.

And now, I have made the worst fool of myself. Maybe Jack does not intend to share me with his brother anymore?

The rumbled conversation resumes, but the up and down tones tell me the conversation is not entirely calm.

The longer I lay unattended on the bed, the greater my resentment grows. How was I supposed to know I should not present? They were both staring at me like they wanted to rut!

I am facing down, but I pull a pelt over my head for good measure at the sound of approaching footsteps. "Go away! You are not welcome here!"

This is a ridiculous statement given it is Jack's home and bedding chamber, but my temper has had an opportunity to fully charge while he has been talking to the other alpha.

An alpha I have just presented my pussy to for ravishment in the most unseemly way.

"Fuck me, is that a nest?"

My ears prick up. That is not Jack's voice. *Fen's* voice. I think I swoon a little. It is for the best I am lying down.

Then I remember that I bared my pussy to him, and now, I feel sick.

I am getting hot under the pelt. But I also don't want to show any of me to any male ever again.

Wait? *Nest?*

"Gods, she has a fucking perfect ass."

That is also not Jack. That is swoon-worthy Fen.

I squeal as a giant hand encloses my ankle. It is only now that I realize I have pulled the pelt over my head and left the rest of me exposed! My scandalously short dress does not cover anything! I am tugged from my poorly crafted hiding with more squeals of outrage. I kick and thrash as he turns me over. Fully ready to maim the male who dares to interrupt my self-pity.

"Hush lass," Jack says, subduing my small fight with alarming ease and all the while purring, which is unfair for he knows I like it well. I am sprawled out on my back, and he has somehow caged my smaller body with his larger one such that my legs are spread open around him. His earthy scent fills my lungs. Being held by him thus turns my body a little squirmy and makes my traitorous pussy clench in anticipation of rutting.

I shoot a glance to the side to find Fen watching, a smirk lighting his handsome face.

Jack speaks, drawing my attention. "I didn't mean to use a harsh tone when you—"

"Presented myself for rutting," I fill in for him, feeling my flushed cheeks heat further.

"Presented yourself for rutting," he agrees. He is now also smirking.

When I glare, his face softens, and he brushes hair from my hot, tear-damped cheeks. "I didn't mean to make light of your embarrassment. You are cursed to look adorable whenever you are cross."

The tenderness in his expression disarms my temper. "I thought you said I must also present to Fen," I say, trying not to think about the other alpha, who is still in our bedding chamber.

"I did," Jack says. I am still reeling from this statement when he lowers his lips to mine, snatching my breath away.

I groan as his mouth moves over mine. My lips part, allowing his tongue to dip inside to tangle with mine. Every kiss is like the first, a heady, drugging sensation that makes me hot, wriggly, and full of urgency.

"Such, a beautiful, perfect little mate," he says between kisses. "So open and giving. You are so beautiful when you present yourself." His lips lower to my throat, sucking against the skin sharply enough that I know it will leave a little mark. It only makes me hotter and sends dampness pooling between my thighs. "My anger was not at you. It was momentary jealousy knowing I must share you."

Share.

The word echoes around my mind as he continues to stoke my arousal one searing kiss at a time.

Shared.

This is not new news, for he told me that he had a younger brother the first day. My own father proposed I could mate with them both, although such couplings are less common in my birth lands.

I always knew about Fen, but it was pushed aside to a distant event in my future. But now that future is here and upon me. Only now, as Fen waits inside our bedding chamber that I realize the full magnitude of what that means. Jack is a powerful, dominant male who needs to rut often. But his brother is all of that too.

My nails rake over firm flesh when thoughts of both these powerful males tending to me makes me extra hot and needy.

"I think my sweet, lusty little beta is not averse to the thought of vigorous rutting by a second mate," Jack says, pausing to gaze down at me through lidded, hungry eyes. "Will you be a good girl for your two masters? Or do you need some time with the strap first to help prepare you to better accept our cocks?"

A small hiss-groan escapes my lips at the mention of the strap. I have felt the strap before, and I do not like it. But there is something in Jack's eyes as he mentions it as a prelude to them both rutting me that makes my tummy clench.

I see his eyes darken.

"The strap it is," he says. "You were close to accepting all of me this morning. I think the strap will help to soften you for the rutting. We will use some oil when the discipline is done, and I will work my fingers deeply." He strokes a finger over my cheek. "We will make you feel good before we get to the rutting so your tight little pussy can better accept our full cocks.

Tomorrow, we will begin the training with the knotted phallus and plug. You will find it a struggle at first, but that can't be helped. Your scent is changing as you become fertile, and you will soon need to take our knot as well. If you are well behaved and accept this necessary preparation, it will not hurt too badly."

I swallow. My stomach turns over at the mention of it not hurting too badly. I admit to being aroused when there is a little discomfort. When Jack thrust deeply this morning, it made me sore inside. It also made my pussy gush, and I come very powerfully.

His eyes do not leave mine. He sees all this. He *knows* I like it when he is a little rough with me—that I come hardest when he rutted me in shameful view of his second alpha over the oak table.

He shuffles back. "Good girl," he says like the matter is decided. His hand encloses the hem of my dress just as I try to tug it over my naked pussy.

"Goddess!" I gasp as he tugs my dress over my head before tossing it to the floor.

My eyes dart to where his handsome brother stands. Fen is staring at my pussy, cheeks flushed, and expression absolutely ravenous. My legs try to snap shut, but I get a smack to my thigh. "Open your fucking legs," Jack growls, spanking me again when I'm not fast enough. "This is my fucking pussy. Now, it is also Fen's. You will open your legs in the presence of your masters, or I will use the fucking strap, and you will get your naughty bottom plugged without the aid of oil."

My legs spring open. My chest heaves, and my whole body flushes.

"How long has it been since you fucked her?" Fen asks, rubbing his jaw absently as he comes to stand to Jack's right. "Her pussy is absolutely drenched."

"I have not fucked her since this morning when you arrived," Jack replies. "She is naturally responsive to an alpha." His eyes narrow. "And she is not averse to a little pain with her pleasure." Leaning down, he plants a fist beside my hip and presses a single thick finger into my wet pussy. "I've no doubt the mention of me plugging her little bottom without oil has further stoked her arousal."

I clench over his finger as if to confirm his wicked assessment.

Fen laughs, a low, pleasing sound. "Did she just clench?"

"She did," Jack confirms, pumping his finger slowly in and out, and making me twitch against the bed. It makes wet noises that grow louder when Jack works his finger from side to side. "She was so fucking tight when I first claimed her. But she has softened nicely under my constant attention." He rocks the finger from side to side then pumps in and out as if emphasizing my openness. "She comes very easily. But there is yet more training needed to make her perfect for our pleasure. Now there are two of us; her poor pussy will need a rest. We must train her to suck our cocks. Her pretty ass is tight. But she is sensitive there and comes powerfully when I have played."

"She will take well to ass rutting," Fen agrees, nodding. "I can see her tummy and pussy clenching at the mere mention of it." He turns to his brother. "How shall we do this?"

Chapter Eighteen

Fen

I feel like I have stepped into a vivid carnal dream. The sweet beta is laid out on Jack's furs, and her slick little pussy is making the filthiest wet sounds as he fingers her. Her eyes don't know where to go. She closes them, opens them, looks at Jack, looks at me, and then closes them again.

"There is yet more training needed to make her perfect for our pleasure," Jack said a short time ago.

Training. I have never been involved in training a lass. I freely admit that I am committed to whatever this entails.

Jack leans up from where he crowds Hazel on the bed.

"I think the lass should be the one controlling your first time together," he says. Taking both Hazel and me by surprise if her shocked gasp is any indication.

She shakes her head. My cock twitches—it couldn't care less how this goes down so long as it fucking goes.

Jack's eyes narrow at her little show of rebellion. He does not suffer insubordination well. I smirk for the lass is yet new to him and has much to learn. "But first, I will use the strap. It will better help you to focus on doing what you are told. And having no attention since this morning will make you very focused." He nudges his head at me. "Go and fetch the strap."

I hear her stammered protests as I leave for the hall, but I'm already halfway into a stupor, and everything is coming through a tunnel.

Mate. The word echoes through my mind as I collect the strap from the hook and return to the bedding chamber. She is standing with Jack. His arm is around her, big hand cupping her pretty plump ass. He is purring, although I see her trembling a little. This is not punishment, and I know Jack will temper the strokes so that they only heat her skin.

Still, it will sting. And if Hazel responds to a bit of pain, as Jack has mentioned, her pussy will soon be drenched, and she will be needy for attention.

For *my* cock, since Jack mentioned she may use me for her pleasure.

As I hand the strap over, Jack takes it with a nod. "I've had second thoughts," he says. "I think you should hold her while I do this."

I suck a sharp breath in. I have not yet touched her. Now, I must hold her while she suffers a firm discipline. My nostrils flare in anticipation of putting my hands on her.

Hazel peeks back at me over her shoulder.

Fuck. That look, her pretty eyes seem to sear into my soul.

I want to be the one using the strap. I want to hold Hazel down and fill her up with my cock and knot until there is nothing between us. Never have I knotted a lass, for I have never had a mate. I want to use her roughly. I want to do things to her that I have never done before.

"Can you be a good girl for us, Hazel? Can you let Fen hold you while I take the strap to your bottom?"

She is still watching me like she wants me to gobble her up. "Yes," she whispers, never taking her eyes from mine. "I can be good for you and Fen."

Caught in a lusty daze, I sit on the bed as Jack coaxes her into position. Her hands rest tentatively on my shoulders. Petting me softly, she bites her bottom lip. Holding her waist gently, my eyes lower to her lush tits. Fuck, she is so soft and sweet. "Good girl," I say. "Put your knees to either side."

She climbs on, her breasts almost in my face until she rights herself. Her little gasp and smirk do not go unnoticed. "It seems our mate has a little brat in her," I say.

Jack chuckles. Her tits jiggle a little as Jack smooths a hand down her back and pauses to pet her ass.

I am fucking mesmerized by her responsiveness.

"Oh!" her little gasp accompanies him swatting her ass with his hand, and my eyes flash to meet hers.

"I wish I had ten sets of eyes," I say. "So that I might look everywhere at once." Her lips tug up in a smile. She gasps again in a way that is half a groan as Jack lands another firm spank.

Lowering my lips to her ear, I whisper, "I can smell your cunt creaming, my needy little beta."

Then a squeal leaves her throat, and she arches in my arms as Jack lands the strap for the first time.

"Goddess! Oh!" She jiggles about most enticingly, throwing a glance over her shoulder at Jack.

"Eyes on Fen, lass," Jack says sternly.

She turns back just as the next strike falls. I nearly fucking come in my pants, watching the rapture contort her face. She squeals, gasps, groans, strains, and arches as Jack administers her loving discipline. I am utterly captivated. I am lost in her pretty eyes as I watch all her emotions play out. Her scent perfumes the air making my mouth water and my cock leak pre-cum. "Good girl," I say. My hands move to her tits that she is all but thrusting into my face. "Do you need me to touch your pretty tits while my brother disciplines you?"

"Yes," she gasps. "Please, yes."

I growl. Jack also growls. We have lost all sense of caution. I cup her breasts just as Jack lands another strike.

"Oh! Goddess, please!" She twitches, pushing her plump tits deeper into my hands.

"Tell Fen what you need, lass," Jack commands. He uses the strap sparingly, stoking her arousal with each careful stroke.

"Please, pinch them. I need you to pinch them!"

I pinch her nipples, and she goes fucking wild, hips thrusting against me.

Another lick of the strap, and I swear she is close to coming.

"Tell him what you fucking need," Jack demands.

"Harder!"

I pinch and squeeze her nipples roughly, and she never once turns away. I am fucking drowning in this tiny, sweet, filthy little beta who the Goddess has created perfectly for us.

"You are not to fucking come," I say. The little imp dares to hiss her displeasure at me. I am so fucking hard, I cannot think straight. Jack told us that Hazel should be the one driving this, but I'm too fucking desperate. "Open my pants and take my cock out."

She squeals as another strike lands. I hear Jack growl at my instruction, but I don't fucking care. Breaking eye contact, she fumbles with my belt, gasping with excitement as she grasps me in her small hands.

I hear the strap drop to the floor. I think Jack is fingering her pussy, and it is driving her wild.

"Yes!" Her hands work my stony cock erratically before she tries to line it with her pussy. "Please, please, please." Planting a hand in the center of my chest, she gives me a push. It's not firm, but I am just as fucking impatient, and I fall back on the bed joggling her about as I shuck my pants down past my hips.

Jack fists her hair, bringing her franticness to a stop as he captures her lips. Her wet little pussy snags my cock, and she sinks slowly, moaning into Jack's mouth.

I breathe. Breathing is all I can do as her hot inner walls surround my length. The rippling heat, the tightness, the slick feeling of being welcomed inside her is utterly sublime. Then she clenches, and I nearly shoot my fucking load.

Jack lifts his head, staring at her flushed lips before he takes in my pained expression. I will not fucking cum like a green whelp just because this is the first time I have had a pussy. Jack smirks before returning his attention to the little beta panting. "Let yourself sink all the way down," he says. "You took my cock all the way up inside this morning. I know you can do it again."

Her thighs tremble where they are braced around my much larger size. Hands fisting at my side, I groan as I stare at her tight pussy stretched obscenely around my thick rod. Then I growl, my dick jerking as I anticipate getting those last few inches inside her hot little pussy.

She sinks, gasps, and sinks some more, only to jerk up again.

"Oh!"

"Good girl," Jack says. "Do that again." His hand collars her throat from behind. He is applying a little pressure, and she sinks deeply again. Her hands plant on me to brace, but Jack gathers them up and holds them to her lower back.

"Goddess," she says, throwing a look over her shoulder at Jack. With her wrists pinned at the small of her back, she has nowhere to brace or hold.

"All. The way. Down," he repeats, his voice the stern one that brokers no dissent.

Her hips move, slowly at first. Up and down, and little gyration with every rise and fall that feels fucking amazing.

"Fuck! She is taking all of me," I say. The sensation of her stretched pussy sliding over the knot is fucking addictive. "Fuck, that feels so fucking good. She is taking me so fucking deep inside her." I was trying not to interfere. I think touching her might send me over the end, but I can't fucking help myself. With a growl of defeat, I palm her tits, pinching and pulling the nipples until her mouth opens on a shocked gasp. "I think you can go deeper, Hazel. Grind your naughty little pussy down."

"No!"

She doesn't like it when it goes extra deep, and she won't fucking grind. Jack fists her hair and forces her deep.

Her squeal is not all pleasure, but her pussy crushes my cock. I feel a hot gush. She is coming. I am coming. We are both fucking coming.

"Ohgodohgodohgod!" she wails.

I grasp her hips to hold her still and tight. Inside her, my knot is swelling. I want to fucking move. I want to force it in and out of her clenching pussy so that it might fully form. It has never fully formed before. I think it might happen now without me thrusting at all.

I can't think straight. My hips jerk erratically, although I am trying to keep them still. My entire focus is on the heady sensation of cum ejecting from my cock, driving my need to slam her up and down.

Then she is snatched away, and I snarl in feral rage.

"You do not fucking knot her yet," Jack snarls back.

He puts her beside me on her hands and knees. She squeals as he slams deep. Hands bracing her hips, he ruts her with barely tempered aggression.

I want to fucking challenge him, but I am also captivated by the rapture contorting her face as he shuttles in and out. I move without thought. My cock is still twitching and streaming cum, and it needs to go somewhere. That somewhere is her open mouth. As I fist her hair, she groans around me. I fuck shallowly into her mouth. She gags and leaks spit over my cock. It is a terrible fucking blow job but also the best I've ever had.

Then Jack is coming, and her wild sucking as she follows him over coaxes my last great gush of cum.

Jack has not knotted her either, I distantly recognize as we collapse together in a heap upon the bed.

I have never shared a bed with a lass I have rutted before. I have never shared a bed with Jack either. Yet it is the most natural thing in the world to trap her tiny, limp body between us where she will be most safe. Her face is in my chest, her back to Jack. I stare at her in sleepy wonder as she continues to twitch and groan.

I like the way she tangles her legs with mine, and the way her plump tits are pressed against my chest. Jack has thrust his thigh between hers, big hand at her hip and nose buried in her hair.

He purrs. I yawn. He used to purr for me when I was a younger boy, and I take comfort from the sound. For the first time in my life, I find myself purring too.

Hazel makes a cute little sigh and snuggles deeper into my chest.

Is this warm feeling spreading through my chest, love? It tickles, feels both heavy and light, and full of contentment. My fingers play in her silky hair. I yawn again.

A funny rumbly noise comes from Hazel. For a moment, I think it might be a purr.

Then my lips tug up as I realize our little beta mate is snoring as she sleeps.

Chapter Nineteen

Jack

Afew days pass, and there have been yet more skirmishes with the Lyon clan, but finally, news has arrived that I have been waiting for.

Soon, this interlude will be over as we seek to keep our clan safe. It has been many years since we suffered such discord. I was uneasy a few years back when the Lyon clan assimilated another clan and claimed their territory. I should have acted at the time, but I had my own problems to deal with. Life is never simple here. Living in the shadow of the mountains as we do, the clans often suffer raiding from the Blighten. Having Orcs decimate our homes is enough. We do not need to fight among ourselves.

Yet we do.

It is strange how such moments bring the past to the fore. After my parents passed to the pox, conflict found our village. My place as the new king was not a given, for I was still a lad of fifteen summers. I killed three men once loyal to my father in the bloodbath that followed. My life and position here is built upon blood. Scars litter my body, old and new, in evidence of who I am and what I am prepared to do.

The Goddess is ever weaving. I do not shy from necessary battles. Ever. I will assuredly not shy away from it now that I have a young mate entrusted to my care.

Hazel is off with the womenfolk today. She has already found a firm friend in Jessa. It heartens me to see her fitting in so well after her terrible introduction to the clan.

Fen cannot stop fucking grinning as we commandeer the hall of my home to meet about the impending war. I want to cuff the cocky fucker, but he is too old for that. Still, the urge does not go away.

"What?" he says, faking affront.

"We will need to begin her training tonight," I say.

Fen's eyes darken. Glen chuckles as he takes a seat to my right. I shoot my second a glare.

He only shrugs. "I have some tips if you need help," he says smugly. The alpha has two beta mates, so I expect he does know a thing or two. Although, I am far from green in such matters.

"I will manage," I say. The training plugs and phallus have arrived. I requested them the day after she arrived, for I had to send a request to the eastern lands where they hold skills in making such things. The small, fur-lined, wooden box is sitting on the table beside the bed. It contains a knotted phallus and three training plugs for her bottom, along with a vial of natural oil to aid the insertion. They are crafted from glass and beautifully smooth. I saw Hazel eying the box curiously last evening when I placed it there. I wonder if she will take a look.

I find myself hoping that she will.

The rattle of the great double doors closing brings me back to the matter at hand as we plan for the war.

Hazel

After a meeting with the warriors this morning, Jack and Fen went out scouting. They are still gone when I return to our home. Today has been spent with Jessa and her mother, weaving blankets ready for when Jessa leaves home. I have not met the beta shifter she is soon to be joined with, but I see the young lass is excited about the coming changes in her life.

As I enter the bedding chamber to wash my hands and face, my eyes shift to the little box resting on the table beside the bed. Jack placed it there last night before joining me in the furs.

I'm curious as to what it is.

It's none of my business, I tell myself as I wash up, but the moment I am done, my eyes drift there again.

My ears prick up, listening for sounds of interruption. I bite my lower lip, knowing I need to have a little peek. Most likely, it is something dull.

I approach the bed with exaggerated casualness, but my eyes are all on the box. It is beautiful, I realize as I near. Ornately carved and lacquered so that it shines in the fading light. It looks like it might hold something valuable, maybe jewels or gems. I have never seen a jewel or treasure, and now, I am twice as curious.

Quite large, it fills half of the small table.

A quick peek confirms no one is about to interrupt me.

Taking the last step, I sit on the side of the bed and lift the lid slowly up.

"Oh."

It is not what I was expecting. There are four strangely shaped items made from beautiful rose-colored glass. Another peek over my shoulder confirms I'm still alone. I lift the smallest one up, watching it sparkle in the light. It resembles an upside-down teardrop, with a stalk and little flared base that I guess might be a stand. An ornament of some kind, I decide.

I put it back, noting that two similarly shaped ones but slightly larger lay inside.

At the end is a larger ornament. This has leather straps attached that pass through an eye on the glass. The straps are very curious. They look a little like a harness for a horse. This ornament looks more like a thick sausage with a wider ridge in the middle.

"Oh!"

I nearly drop it in my haste to put it back, snapping the lid shut with a bang.

"Goddess!!!" Heat fills my cheeks. *"Gods, you are tight enough to strangle my cock,"* Jack said that first night as he claimed me in my father's cottage. *"I will order an appropriate training phallus when we get home."*

Standing, I pace, wringing my hands and willing myself to find some measure of calm. "Oh, why did I look?" I mutter and set about pacing some more. Why is my pussy growing damp at the thought of him using them on me? The largest one is for my pussy. The smaller ones must be intended to stretch my ass.

"Goddess save me from the alpha's depravity!" I wail.

"The Goddess will not save you, lass," a voice says ominously behind me.

I spin, finding Jack in the entrance to our bedding chamber. Fen is at his side.

"Do you think she looked?" Fen asks, smirking.

"Aye," Jack says. "I think that she did." Then he crooks his finger at me. "Come, lass, it's time for some discipline before we acquaint you with your new plugs."

Chapter Twenty

Fen

As Jack has explained, there is yet more training required before Hazel can take our full knot.

"Over you go, lass," Jack says. He sits on the side of the bed and pats his knee encouragingly.

"No!"

I smirk at her defiance. Already naked, for we have already divested her of her dress, she presents her charms to our view. Why she fights any of this is a mystery. The lass takes to rutting and loving discipline in ways that blow my mind.

She squeals as Jack snags her wrist. He gets that gleam in his eye that I am becoming familiar with as he hauls her over his lap. Here, he sets about disciplining her with the palm of his hand. Her bottom soon flushes a cherry red.

The little bit of complaint and wriggling is deeply captivating.

"I have barely started, lass," Jack says between firm spanks.

Her bottom jiggles with each strike, and her arousal perfumes the air. On the furs beside Jack are three different-sized plugs, smoothed so that they can be inserted into her bottom.

Training plugs, Jack calls them, because she is particularly small and tight.

A final one has a knot which she will have to take inside her pussy.

But first, we will use the smaller plugs for her bottom.

I have taken many lasses that way over the years since I matured. But I have never been responsible for breaking them in for this pleasure. I am deeply aroused by the prospect of being involved in the training. Jack has always forbidden me from taking the younger lasses, for he says I'm too rough.

I *am* too rough but will temper it for the sweet beta I'm determined to make my mate.

"Oh, please!"

The last spank was particularly firm. My cock is stone-hard within my hide pants. This is all new to me. Until now, pleasure was about sticking my dick somewhere and thrusting until I come. Now, I realize that pleasure is also about making a lass squirm.

"Submit to your discipline," Jack growls, spanking even harder. "Do I need to take the strap to your naughty bottom before you accept your lowly place before your masters?"

Gods, I swear I nearly empty my balls watching his stern way with her. I am dominant too, and I like obedience. I did not realize that I also like this small fight and the rebelliousness she is displaying. I like the thought of taming and training her for my pleasure. I like the idea of learning how to gain her submission through this loving form of discipline.

I also want to rut her pussy with a desperateness that has me fearing I will unman myself inside my pants.

"Oh!" she falls limp and sets to sobbing.

I am entranced by her pretty tears. Her legs fall open a little, and I can see her pussy is glistening as she finally allows Jack to finish her stern discipline without struggle.

His spanks lower to her sensitive sit-spot, and it rouses a little of her spirit.

"Open your legs wider," he demands. His spanks land slower but with no less force. Her legs pop open wide, and he pauses to smooth his big hand over her inflamed skin. I don't blink as I stare at her little puffy pussy slit. Before I returned, Jack had shaved all her hair away from her pussy so that she is smooth. I can see the smears of her juices coating the tops of her slim thighs. "I'm going to spank your pussy for the last few," he says ominously.

I swallow.

Surely that must sting a great deal for a lass is sensitive there. But for reasons I do not fully understand, I think it will also give her pleasure.

Especially Hazel, who is not averse to a little pain.

"Hold your legs still for me while I do this," he says. "That way, I will know you can be a good girl while we plug your little bottom hole. If you are naughty about this, I will need to spank you some more."

Her little pussy clenches at his words, glistening with her arousal. She mumbles something I cannot hear. I smirk, thinking about the impossible choice he has given her. She does not want us to plug her bottom, but she has experienced a stern discipline, and she does not want more of that either.

These last few spanks on her pussy will be a challenge for her to endure. Instinctively, I understand this is part of her training to make her perfect for our needs. We will both need to rut her often, and she is responding to Jack's discipline and firm demands.

"Hold very still," he warns.

The next three strikes come in quick succession against her sensitive pussy.

I swear there is no blood left anywhere in my body but my dick when she squeals, straining to hold her legs perfectly open and endure.

"Good lass," he says, sinking a thick finger into her gushing pussy, and turning her sounds into needy whimpers. "You took that so well. I'm going to make sure you come just as soon as you accept the plug."

His finger makes a delicious wet sound as he pumps it slowly in and out. His head lifts, and his eyes meet mine before returning to the bed. "I think we will start with the medium one," he says.

Her shocked gasp of outrage on learning that he is skipping the smallest one brings a smirk to my lips. "Hush, lass," he says. "This is not for you to decide. We shall use the medium one for now. Once you have had a little time for the plug to stretch you, we will leave the smaller one in while you go about your chores. You will find it much easier to bear if you have taken the larger one, first."

"Use plenty of the oil, Fen," he says to me. "It will help it to slide in."

I stumble in a trance to the bed where the small bottle of special oil and plugs wait. Now that I am closer, I can see how drenched she is. "The lass has responded perfectly to the discipline," I say.

"She has been a good girl for us," he says, pulling his finger from her little pussy and giving her inflamed bottom a little tap. "Up you get, Hazel. You will bend over the bed for this so that Fen can get to you easily."

I catch a glimpse of her tear-stained face as she rises. He pauses to brush her hair from her cheeks, cuddling her to him and filling his big hand with her hot little bottom. She twitches and gasps. If I weren't already halfway in love with her, the cuteness has clinched it.

"You have felt my finger there. This will not be so different," Jack says, encouraging her to get into position over the side of the bedding platform. She sends a furtive glance at me before burying her face in the furs. "Reach your hands back," Jack instructs. "Pull yourself open like I have taught you."

I shoot him a glare. The fucker is doing this on purpose to make me lose my fucking load.

Her little hands tremble as she pulls her bottom cheeks open. I can see her little hole clenching, for our sweet little beta is very tense. My fingers shake, too, as I unstopper the bottle. "How is this to be done?" I look to Jack for direction; I don't want to fuck this up and hurt her. "Should I work the oil in with my fingers first?"

"Yes," he says. "Use plenty of oil and open her. Then you can push the plug in."

Her fingers turn white against the heated pink flesh of her bottom. She hisses as I trickle the oil and press my middle finger slowly in.

"Oh!" her hands tremble. I can feel her bottom clenching over my finger. "Fuck, she is tight," I say. "I don't think my cock will ever go in here."

"She will learn to accept it," Jack says, tone brokering no discussion. After I work a little oil in, I pet over the sensitive area near the entrance before sinking my finger in again. This time she clamps tightly over my finger when I press it inside. I share a look with Jack, he grins back. "She comes very powerfully when I pet her little bottom. She will come to enjoy our cocks here. Maybe more than she enjoys the rutting of her pussy." He strokes gentle fingers through her hair when she frets a little at this news.

I work more oil inside, rubbing all around the little puckered entrance before thrusting my finger inside two or three times. Soon, her channel is slick, and I force my second finger in.

"Oh!"

She releases her bottom cheeks. Instinctively, I thrust my fingers deeper to keep her still as Jack grasps a fistful of her hair. "Good girl. Just lay there and let Fen do as he needs to."

I thrust in and out. She is very tight and won't stop clenching. But she is also slippery with the copious oil, and her small struggles do not stop me.

"I think she is ready for the plug," I say. The truth is, I am fucking desperate to fill her pussy, and I think that will come around sooner once I have seated the plug.

Jack nods. I ease my fingers out, watching as her little bottom hole winks and clenches from the stretching in the most enticing way. It is not until the plug is next to her bottom entrance that I realize how big it is. I pour a little more oil over it for good measure before pushing the polished tapered tip in.

"Oh! It is too big," she wails, bringing a smirk to my lips.

"Naughty, lass. It is not yet as thick as my fingers were. Do you need some more time over Jack's lap before you can be good for us?"

She quietens, although there is a great deal of twitching when it nears the widest point.

"Bear down, lass," Jack says. "If you can push back, it will be easier on your bottom."

Noticing her bottom clench, I twist the plug. I think she likes the feeling, although I can see it is a struggle for her to take.

I like that it is a struggle. I cannot deny that I'm aroused by the thought of tossing the plug aside and forcing her to take my cock in this tight place right now. I'm a little rougher about the task than I might have been in my enthusiasm and the plug pops in.

"Goddess!" Her body goes completely stiff, and she emits a sharp guttural moan. "Ohgodohgodohgod!"

"Fuck!" I mutter. Her bottom keeps clenching rhythmically over the little plug, making it move about. "Fuck, she is coming. I need to fuck her."

My fingers fumble the ties of my hide pants. I don't even wait to seek Jack's permission. I can think of nothing beyond the need to feel her pussy gripping me under this powerful climax.

"Good girl," Jack says, holding her still against the furs as I line my cock up with her pussy.

I thrust.

"Fuck! Fuck! Fuck!" I growl as my hips snap back and forth. "She is already coming. She is coming all over my cock." The plug makes her clenching pussy strange. I can feel it every time I plow her cunt. I grit my teeth. The pleasure is intense. I am so fucking hard, it's like I want to come too much, and I cannot fucking come!

Each stroke bangs the flared base of the plug and drives a gasp or squeal of pleasure from her lips. I am sweating. My balls are tight to the point of pain. I am going to empty a bucket inside her when I come. I land a sharp spank against her ass. "Clench me again." She wails her protest, but another sharp spank sees her do as she is told.

"Ahhh!!! Fuck!" The gush of cum exploding from the tip of my cock is so intense, I almost forget myself and fill her with my knot. "Fuck! Fuck! Fuck!" My hips jerk erratically. "She is coming again," I gasp in wonder. "The lass is made for rutting."

She is still fucking coming—I am still coming too—but I'm fighting the urge to slam my knot in, so I ease from her hot cunt.

"Fuck!" I mutter as a gush of come pours out. I want to push my cock in again despite it being too intense, for I do not like the sight of all my seed spilling out. I don't get a chance. Jack snatches her up and fills her in a single thrust.

I stagger to my feet, half in a stupor as my brother fucks her hard and fast.

She squeals after a particularly savage thrust, and I think he has just found her limit.

Jack

No sooner does Fen stagger away than I am taking his place and spearing her gushing cunt. I suffer a compelling notion that plugging the hole will stop the wastage, but I'm also riveted by her clenching bottom. Her pussy clamps over my length so strongly, I forget everything, including breathing for an extended period.

"She has taken to this so well," I growl between thrusts. The fullness and the sensation of her clenching is fucking amazing. I think I am going to keep her plugged all the time.

The poor lass is wailing and coming near constantly. I want to last, but too soon, I'm spewing deep.

"She really enjoyed the plug," Fen says as I am still gasping and fighting the urge to bury my bulging knot. "She is a natural. What a treasure we have found."

I don't even need to tell her to clench since she cannot fucking stop.

She is limp on the bed by the time I'm done filling her with my seed. Fen is petting her hair and telling her how good she is taking her masters' cocks.

She is still twitching as I ease from her hot passage, sending cum splattering over the wooden floor. "Oh!" she makes a grab for her well-used pussy as more and more cum drips and gushes out.

A sharp spank to her bottom, and I gather her wrists so she cannot touch.

"Oh, my tummy aches!"

I look to Fen, seeing the darkening of his face. With her wrists clasped in my hand, I finger her pussy, thrusting vigorously to help her push the excess out. "Keep your hands out of the way," I caution before releasing her wrists. Reaching under and gently massage her belly. "There," I say. "We have filled you all up. Be good for me while I do this, and it will not ache so much."

"Mmnnn!" She comes again, the little plug in her bottom twitching with the contractions, and a great gush of cum is ejected.

She might have squirted. It is hard to tell. After, she lays panting.

"We best take the plug out while we work the knotted phallus in," Fen says, stirring me from the arresting image of our well-ravished mate.

Smoothing a hand over her bottom, I grasp the base of the plug and gently pull.

"Goddess!"

The naughty lass immediately grips.

"Relax your bottom," Fen commands, giving her bottom a couple of sharp smacks that set her wailing and make her clench twice as hard. I have no choice but to pull the plug out roughly.

She tries to clamp her hands over her bottom. "Oh! I am open! You have broken me!"

"Hush, lass," Fen says, gathering her hands and pressing a finger into the little winking bottom hole. She immediately clamps down.

"Oh, I want to come again!" Her gasped words send blood pooling into my dick. "Oh! Please, don't plug me again. I do not like it!" She wails this between groans as she humps herself back onto Fen's finger.

I can't decide whether to laugh at her ridiculous denial of her joy and needs, or to thrust Fen's inadequate finger aside and make her scream with pleasure as she takes my cock inside her needy little bottom hole.

Fen's face is an image of rapture. Cheeks flushed; he is riveted by our little mate as she works herself on his finger. "Good girl," Fen says. "Get yourself off if you need to. This is natural for a mate claimed by two alphas. You will soon be as eager to feel our hardened length in here."

"I can't take any more!" she wails.

Fen finally eases his finger out.

"I beg to differ, lass," I say, smirking. "You have not stopped fucking coming."

Hazel

I'm utterly numb as my bottom twitches and clenches in little echoes that spark into the emptiness. I lie limp on the bed, face down. They are both purring. Fen presses a kiss to my hot cheeks while his hand cups my bottom, clenching over the smarting flesh.

Then I feel the thick blunt intrusion pressing into the entrance of my pussy. I start, finding hands holding me securely against the furs even as they purr. I don't think I can take more. But they are not giving me a choice. Having seen the thick knotted phallus, I assuredly do not want to hold it inside me. It has not gotten very deep when it flares.

"Hold her thighs," Jack instructs his brother. "The lass is going to be naughty about this."

Leaning down, Fen takes a firm hold of my thighs, pinning me open and pressing me securely to the side of the bed.

I strain, but there is not a bit of give.

The pressure grows and grows, making my pussy flutter. This is unnatural. A knot is not meant to be pushed inside. At least, I do not think it is.

"Stop clenching, lass," Jack says.

"I can't."

Then he pushes, and it pops inside. I'm very full and grip even harder.

"I think I'm going to come," I groan. My body is exhausted from all their attention, and I assuredly cannot endure more.

"Let yourself come," Fen says. His hand slides under me, and rough fingers find my clit.

"Please! No. I cannot come around it!"

But I do, and it is such a dark, twisty climax that I groan and strain. It aches deep inside as my pussy squeezes the unyielding phallus.

In the aftermath, I lie there twitching. Pussy stuffed beyond comfort.

"Good girl," Fen says, stroking my hair. "You took that so well."

The straps are passed under my body, tightening the beastly thing into place. I try to close my legs now that they are no longer holding me. A groan erupts from my chest when even this slight movement makes me clench over the thick knot.

"Careful, lass," Jack says, gathering me into his arms. The light has faded as clouds pass over. They purr, settling me between them with my cheek to Jack's chest. Behind me, Fen presses his chest to my back. Hands smooth over my skin and lips kiss. "Once you have calmed, we will let you have a rest with the knot inside you. Fen will be back later to take it out."

The straps keep the phallus firmly in place. I dare not move since it makes me squeeze around the thickness.

I don't like the feeling. I'm open, and I cannot imagine how it will be once they take it out.

But I am also exhausted, and I drift to sleep between them.

Chapter Twenty-One

Fen

Today I must leave to talk to the Halket clan as we prepare for the war.

My morning starts with me encouraging Hazel to climb on top and ride my face. She is still shy about such things. I think that is half of what makes her wet pussy leak over my chin. She comes with a deep groan, and little *ohgod* noises tumble out of her mouth.

When she's done twitching, I pull her down my body and line my cock up before forcing her to take my full length. She is still fucking tight, and Jack has forbidden me from plugging her with my knot.

"Clench," I say. I have her hips in my hands. Her tits jiggle about all over the place as I slam her up and down. Her small hands brace against my stomach, trying to find stability. Goddess, I could wake up to this every fucking day. Now that I think about it, I do.

Soon, she will be fertile.

I am desperate to come, but I want her to come with me just one more time. "Rub your clit," I say. She groans as she does as instructed, making her pussy clench around me in the most arresting way. I will never get enough of her hot cunt.

We come together, her with mumbled nonsense and me with harsh growls.

In the aftermath, we breathe heavily. Instinctively, I purr for her. Well sated, she collapses against my chest.

Jack left while it was dark. But it is still early, and through the shuttered window, weak sunlight peeps in. We cuddle and nap. I play with her hair, letting my other hand roam over her luscious ass. My cock jerks where it is still buried inside her. Her hiss tells me she is not ready to go again.

"Did I hear Jack taking your pretty mouth this morning before he left?" I ask. I know that he did, but I like asking her just to see her reaction.

She fidgets before mumbling, "Yes."

I smile. Now that there are two of us, her little pussy gets quite sore. But she is being trained to suck our cocks, so there is plenty of that. Although she is not very good at swallowing and spits it out half the time. I admit to finding it amusing when she spits out Jack's cum. His eyes get that glazed rage thing, and he scoops it up and forces her to take it from his hand.

Sometimes she does, and sometimes, she is a brat about it. Life is never dull.

As per Jack's instructions, she must tell us if she wants to do that instead of rutting. I admit I enjoy making her pussy all sore then asking her for more, knowing that she has no choice but to take it in her mouth.

"What are your plans today?" I ask.

"Jessa has been teaching me about local plants. We are going to make some balm for wounds."

The news of her task is a cold douse over the moment. I

know why Jessa is tasked to make more balm. Today, we have plans that will lead toward war. Soon, I will leave for my own duties. Before I am home again, we will have challenged the Lyon clan.

In war, you cannot afford to show weakness.

I do not want war, but we have no fucking choice. They have attacked our hunting parties. Yesterday, a hunter returned severely injured—he may lose a leg. Jack is determined to see the Lyon clan well punished. But war is never easy. And once upon that path, some of us may die.

As my sweet little beta lays limp over me, I wish we were not warring. In the past, I would've relished an opportunity to battle with my enemy. But now, I see things differently.

"I need to go," I say. But as I try to rise from the bed, Hazel clings and begins to sob. The feelings that assault me are foreign. I've never cared this deeply about a person, nor have I worried for them in this way. "It will be fine," I say. She is yet new to our community and our warring ways. We need to send a strong message to the other clan if we want to survive.

I want to do more than fucking survive. I'm a warrior first and foremost, and I will see our community thrive. There is yet more clinging and sobbing as I try to put her away, and it breaks me apart. Perhaps she is thinking about her late husband who died while at war. Maybe she is thinking about things I do not know. "The Goddess gives, and the Goddess takes," I say as I wipe tears from her cheeks with the pads of my thumbs. For so long, it felt like the Goddess only took from me, but in Hazel, she has also given. "It is our duty to live our life in accordance with the ancient laws. You are not yet with child, but you will be soon if the Goddess wills it. I would not have our babe born into a time of uncertainty. Our clan must be strong so that you and the babe will be safe. We do not seek conflict, but some-times, it will come for us. There are rules which the Lyon clan broke. I could've watched on. I could've let them take a lass from another clan. It had naught to do with me. But I do not think the Goddess favors those who can turn such a blind eye. I think she favors those who are noble in their cause. I think she respects a warrior who would not stand by while a lass was raped and whether the lass was a member of his clan or not."

She nods her head, her face downcast so that I can't see her eyes. I tip her chin, and her hazel eyes, full of tears, search mine. "I do not want a man to come here and tell me that you are gone," she says. "I have felt that before, and I cannot live through it again."

My heart softens toward her. This young lass has already been married and lost a mate. But I am not that mate.

"I will not die," I say. "I promise, we will return. But there is no safety in cowardice. Sometimes, war needs to be done."

Hazel

Great sadness wells up inside me as I watch Fen ready to leave. He pulls his pants up, tightening a belt around his waist. Boots are slipped onto his feet. Leather straps are slipped over his head to crisscross his torso diagonally, which holds pouches and two knives. Finally, he slings a bag over his shoulder before gathering his ax from where it rests against the storage chest sitting at the bottom of the bed.

He may be young, but he is proud. I am proud of him too. That he stopped a lass from being raped speaks of his noble mindset. Before I came to Ralston, I did not understand the ways of the barbarian clans. I imagined them to be brutish people. In some ways, they are. But I have discovered that they are far more complex people. I'm worried about Fen, just as I am worried about Jack. Even if it means war, and that tragedy will come into my life once more, I'm glad he saved the lass.

Maybe the Goddess will choose to take Fen to her side because she loves him well for this noble deed. Or perhaps the Goddess will decide to let him stay with me so that we might grow old together and have many babes.

I will pray for the latter.

Returning to the bed, he catches my face between his strong hands and kisses me on the lips.

But all too soon, he draws back, and I watch him go with sad eyes. The room falls quiet. Between my legs is a little achy. And I can feel the stickiness where he has cum. When I press my fingers to my lips, I can pretend *his* lips are still there.

Rising, I head for the table where the bowl and jug of water rests. Pouring water into the bowl, I lean over to wash my hands and face. I don't know where Jack went earlier, but it is something else to do with the war, and I worry about him. Now that Fen is also gone, I worry about them both.

But there are things to be done. I slip my tunic over my head and my shoes onto my feet. Leaving the bedding chamber, I snatch an apple from the bowl resting on the great oaken table and head down the wooden steps in search of Jessa.

When I enter the little hut where the drying herbs and roots are kept, a few other women are present. The mood is somber. It seems I am not the only one who worries. Jessa greets me with a weak smile. The young beta woman is much enamored with Brandon. Yesterday, I met the beta shifter Jessa will soon be bonded to. He is Fen's best friend and has similarly left for the war.

"Eh, look at you lot," an older lady says. "They are hale men. They will do what needs to be done and return to us, have no fear. Goddess willing, they will have little need of care. But some might need treatment upon their return. So best we make sure we have plenty of balm and bandages ready, so we can see to them swiftly."

I busy myself in the process. There are many stages and exact measures to be made as I grind herbs and crush roots. Then I mix them together with a bit of water as instructed. I am no stranger to medicinal herbs. My mother taught me much. But they have different plants and roots here, and I am learning anew.

The day passes slowly, and the sun sets as we pack up what we have prepared. Some women have babes, children, and husbands who are farmers here, and they return to their homes. But Jessa does not want to return home. She has five siblings who will demand her attention. She tells her parents that she will stay with me, and we leave together, walking the small distance from Ralston to where the sacred pool and portal are found.

The site holds terrible memories. It was here that Nola sought mischief. But it is also a site where the Goddess listens to her people's prayers, and I have many prayers to give.

"Has anyone ever come through?" I ask.

"No," Jessa says. "My grandma told me it was a lost one. That it goes to nowhere, and that nowhere leads here. But the Goddess listens well. I have prayed here many times."

Kneeling side by side, we close our eyes and pray.

I speak to the Goddess through my thoughts.

I entreat her to send Jack and Fen home to me.

I beg her to give me a babe when I am next fertile.

I tell her all the ways I shall cherish the life she might choose to give us. I tell her how I am well practiced at caring for my mates and our children. Whether she listens, I will never know. There are many villages and cities and peoples in the world, and I dare say some have far more pressing concerns than mine.

Dusk has fallen by the time we return to the hall of my

home. I note a few of the younger warriors who have remained carry weapons as they walk in pairs on patrol.

I have never seen that before, and it unnerves me.

A young warrior instructs us to close and bolt the hall door for the night.

Jessa and I eat a cold supper.

And then we wait.

Chapter Twenty-Two

Fen

When I leave home, there is a heaviness in the center of my chest. Usually, under the threat of war, I feel a nervous kind of anticipation, and I cannot wait for it to fucking begin. Things are different since I met Hazel.

Brandon is waiting when I emerge from the house and take the wooden steps down to Ralston Square.

"Fuck," he says, smirking. "You are a miserable fucker this morning."

I shoot him a glare. "You have no reason to talk," I say. "Aren't you and Jessa about to take your vows?"

He grunts but does not dispute the recent change in his status. I know that Brandon is excited about joining with Jessa, even though he pretends not to be. They have been making eyes at one another for a while now. And this despite Jessa's

195

father threatening to castrate Brandon if he touched the lass before she came of age.

Then there is that fight he got into with the bastard from the Lyon clan. A man doesn't take such steps without strong reasons.

We had plans to build a cottage for them when this nonsense with the Lyon clan began. It is the way of people here that we will all work together to create a new home when a young couple comes together. And whether it is the vows of matrimony between two betas or the claiming when an alpha takes a mate.

We walk together to where our horses wait. Three other warriors will ride with us, the rest having traveled with my brother. Jack says I have a hot head and history with the Halket clan.

Which is a fair point.

He also says that a man and clan do not blunder into war. That we need alliances in place.

So Jack has left for more distant negotiations, while I will go with Brandon and three other warriors to speak with Karry, the king of the Halket clan.

I would much rather be the one going to the more distant clan. To any clan but the Halket. But alas, this is my own fault for my mischief with Eric. I have a mate now, and I must step up to my duties in the clan, Jack says.

Our travel passes without incident through the forests. When the sun breaks through gaps in the canopy, I feel its warmth against my shoulders. The kind of day better spent lazing in the furs with your mate rather than dealing with an impending war.

Our pace is fast where possible, but we slow the horses to a walk as we arrive at the river where a ford allows us to cross. As our horses trot through the water, it casts up a great spray.

"What are you going to say?" Brandon asks as we emerge onto the other side.

"I am going to talk plainly," I say.

"Are you going to apologize?" he asks. "For that business with you and Gwen?"

"I am not going to fucking apologize," I say, glaring at Brandon. He does not know me or is baiting me to even ask this. "It is Eric's own fault for being slow about it. Happen, I did him a service helping the matter along."

Brandon chuckles. "Not sure Eric will consider it in the same light."

I think Brandon might be right.

Our discussion ends when I notice a couple of Halket warriors. They are lying upon the ground peering over a low, craggy bluff. I pull my horse to a stop. "Eric?"

"Get down from the fucking horse," Eric hisses.

I don't like his fucking tone. I'm about to tell him as much when I notice Gwen at his side along with half a dozen warriors. Gwen turns to glare at me—she is usually an even-tempered lass.

Dismounting, we tie the horses off a small distance from the edge. The Halket warriors turn back, watching something through the trees.

Keeping tread light, we creep the short distance to join them at the edge.

"Has he claimed you yet?" I ask Gwen as I crouch between her and Eric. It never hurts to give it another push if the fool is still being slow.

"He tried," she says. Her face colors, and she smirks. "But he needed a bit of help."

I laugh. Eric punches me in the arm and glares at me. "Shut the fuck up," he says. "This is not the time for fucking around. And best you move from between my mate and me, or

I will finish what I started last time you got in my fucking way."

I raise both hands in the universal sign of surrender and squat-crawl to the other side of Eric. I can be an asshole sometimes, but I don't joke about mates. "About fucking time," I mutter. Then I'm all business, for I see what they are looking at. "Is that Danon?"

Below, the Lyon warriors have dismounted. Their horses are tethered to one side. We have the vantage of higher ground since the landscape here is rocky with great crumbling boulders that form peaks and troughs.

Danon. A year has passed since I last saw the alpha son of the Lyon clan king. He's a tall, powerful male. My feelings toward him are nothing like the playful mischief I engage in with Eric. Danon's father is a cruel bastard, and his son, cut from the same stone. "What the fuck are they doing on your lands?"

"I do not fucking know," Eric says. "But they're not here for diplomatic reasons, like you. And I doubt they have come to apologize."

"I also am not coming to apologize," I point out.

Eric rolls his eyes. "I am not fucking delusional. The day you apologize for anything is the day the sky turns green. I admit," he says, looking a bit sheepish. "I should've claimed Gwen before." His scowl turns fierce. "I still want to fucking end you for covering her in your cum. But I hear you have a mate now, and for her sake, I will restrain myself from such a path. Also, my father has forbidden it since we already have one war."

"You are at war then?" I ask, returning my attention to the Lyon warriors. What the fuck are they staring at on the ground? Negotiating and strengthening our alliance was, after all, the reason I was coming here today. It seems Eric and I are beginning the discussion early. "How many are there? Why have you not moved them on?" I ask. Although, this is not far into Halket lands. Given the ease of crossing the river at the nearby ford, this is a common pathway between the clans.

"My father ordered us to watch and observe unless the Lyons seek trouble or near our village. He has gone to speak to the Baxters today," Eric says. "He believes the Lyons are planning an attack after they sent our envoy back tied to his horse dead. My father is an honorable king. He does not seek conflict. We must live with the Lyon bastards as our neighbors. But they took a lass promised to a warrior against her will. Her intended is furious that she was taken thus, but prepared to challenge the Lyon warrior who claimed her in a fair fight. The Lyon clan's response was to send the envoy back dead."

My frown deepens. "We have skirmished with them several times since I caught them trying to snatch a second lass," I say.

"What lass?" Eric asks. "One of yours?"

"No, one of yours. A few days after—" Given this is a diplomatic meeting albeit in an unlikely place, I try to find a tactful way to say it was *after I come all over Gwen*. But I'm struggling for terms that won't put him in a rage.

"Gwen," he offers, eyes narrowing like he is thinking about bloodying me again.

"Yes, after the incident with Gwen. Four of them gave chase and caught a lass. They intended to rut and claim her there. It was not so far from your village." This sees me cop another scowl. As Brandon pointed out at the time, we were trespassing after Eric had bluntly told me a few days earlier to 'fuck off his lands'. "They slapped her to quieten her down. Did no lass return with such a mark?"

"Ellen," Gwen says, anger glittering in her voice. "I thought it was her mother who is known to have a temper on her. The poor lass has not had a good life. Happen she was terrified to speak up lest her witchy mother beat her again. She is of age, but her mother refuses to let her mate since she uses the lass as a slave. It's time your father stepped in and found Ellen a mate who will cherish and protect her. She will come and live with us until this can be settled. That way, I may vet any male who petitions for her."

"She will not fucking live with us," Eric says hotly. "We are newly mated and have newly mated needs. Then there are your other two mates. My home is already fucking crowded!"

"She will stay with us," Gwen says, eyes narrowing in a way that does not bode well for Eric's rutting prospects in the near future.

I chuckle, finding great mirth at Eric's expense.

"Fuck!" That is a Brandon kind of fuck.

We all turn back to the forest where the warriors are hoisting something up. A wooden cage? No, a wooden *framework* is being hoisted into the trees. In the middle is a body. A freshly killed body that is dripping with blood. I see the dyed leather so typical of the Halket clan, and I know the man—now dead—is from there.

Eric roars. A fearsome warrior already, when enraged, he is demonic in his power.

Inside, I feel the shifting as blood pounds in anticipation. This here and now is the beginning of the war.

There is no hesitation. The challenge has been issued. The Lyon warriors turn as we charge, drawing weapons and shouting to each other to ready. We meet, crashing like two great waves into one another. Blades strike, meeting screams, and snarled fury.

This is me, a dirty, gritty, cleaving monster that takes down enemies with the flashing curve of ax or fist.

Some fall.

Some scatter.

And some stand and fight.

I punch, cleave, batter at those who stand in my way. At my side, the snarls and growls tell me that Brandon has joined the fight.

Then I see him, *Barry,* the fucker who slapped a helpless lass and who sought to claim and rut her. For Barry, I will not make it quick. I batter his sword away. Swinging my curving ax down, I hamstring him as he tries to flee. He stumbles, gets his good leg under him, and tries to limp away.

Until I hamstring his other leg.

Around me, the sounds have turned from the frenzy of a skirmish to the moaning penance as dying men beg for mercy.

Barry begs. Dragging himself along the ground, legs limp and useless. He is bleeding, leaving a dark stain over the loamy forest ground. He will not last long—I pause my pursuit and smirk.

"We should string the bastard up," Brandon says as he comes to stand beside me—human and naked. Barry is still trying to crawl, but it is slower and weaker now.

"No," I say, never taking my eyes from the fallen man whose begging has turned pitiful. "He will die slower this way."

A call comes from behind, and I turn to find Eric has subdued Danon. The Lyon alpha snarls and curses as they bind him and set him to his knees.

"There will be retaliation," I say.

Eric nods, face and torso dripping with blood, although I think none of it is his. "There will be more than retaliation," he says. Stalking forward, he punches Danon in the face sending the bound alpha sprawling. "They wanted war. War is what they shall get."

Pivoting, he calls to a nearby warrior. "Cut my father down."

It is then I remember the dead man strung up like a gruesome offering.

As I look up, cold sweeps my spine.

The dead man is Karry, the Halket king.

Gwen wails in sorrow. I note the tear tracks merging with the blood on Eric's face. And I see the deadly calm that has settled over the bloody clearing.

Eric, through cruel circumstances, is no longer the son of a king.

Chapter Twenty-Three

Hazel

Disinclined toward sleep and full of worry, Jessa and I go to the bedding chamber where we lay together chatting about this and that. Through words, we find a distraction from our concerns. We talk about herbs, the ladies of the clan, the children we plan to have, and the men we have both come to love.

Night falls, and still our warriors are not back.

"I met Fen a long time ago," I say. "My father is a blacksmith. Jack and Fen visited him from time to time." I smile as I remember this fond memory. "We sat together by the river, and while there, he stole my first kiss. I was thirteen at the time."

She giggles and twists on her side to face me. "What happened?"

"Naught," I say. "Jack called Fen in that stern voice of his, and they left."

She rolls onto her back and stares at the ceiling. "I kissed a lad once who was not Brandon."

I gasp in shock. Then Jessa giggles prettily, and I laugh too.

"So, Brandon is not your only love?" I ask.

"I have found lads handsome before," she says like she is far older and wiser than she really is. "But he is from another clan." Her voice turns sad. "And their clan and ours do not mix so well. But I love Brandon with all my heart, and I had all but forgotten about it until you made mention of Fen."

The room has darkened, and that heightens my awareness of the tone of her voice.

There was wistfulness when she spoke of the other man.

It is the way of the clans that sharing is as common as a pairing. I wonder if that might have been Jessa's fate were the other clan in better alliance with Ralston. I wonder what the clan's name is, but I only know a few, and it would likely not mean much to me even if I were to ask.

And Jessa cares for Brandon. Every time Brandon is near, she blushes prettily. Jessa has been smitten with the handsome shifter beta for a good while, from what I have learned. He is a little older than her and experienced in life. Her father has been strict about her not being alone with the beta male until she is of age. Given all the rutting that happens in Ralston—and I have seen Brandon sneak off with a lass or two—I can see that it has been hard for Jessa as she grows into becoming a woman.

I yawn, feeling tiredness battle against the unease fluttering inside my tummy. Poor Jessa. Finally, when her father accepts Brandon, this business with the Lyon clan has begun.

"Do you know where the house for you will be built?" I ask.

"On the eastern side, next to my parents' home," she says. "Mama says she will be able to help me when I get with a child. But I also think she is anticipating me helping with all my brothers and sisters."

There is a smile in her voice. She likes to grumble about her younger siblings, but she also loves them dearly.

I wish I had a mother still who could help me when I come to have a babe of my own. My brothers and sisters are either grown up or yet live with my uncle and aunty. My oldest brother is a soldier in the army and battles the Blighten far away on the other side of the great sea. I miss how it was when my siblings were little. I think that was the happiest time of my life before my mother passed, and there were five of them all running around up to mischief.

I miss my father, the gruff old goat that he is; how I love him dearly. I worry for him alone in that old cottage full of memories of happier times. He is a good father, both before and after my mother passed. There was a time when we were all deep into our grieving where he was not himself. But when there are little ones who need love and attention, you must pick yourself up.

"They are very late," I say softly, for we have fallen quiet.

"Aye," Jessa says.

The unsaid words of worry float between us as I drift into sleep.

A hand closing over my mouth stifles my scream. Troubled dreams fade as my mind rushes to alert. I fight. I may be a beta, but I still know my mates' scent and feel. The cruel hands that grasp me are assuredly neither Jack nor Fen. Around me are the sounds of a scuffle, hissed orders, and low curses. I am still on the bed and see a jumble of moving shapes and shadows.

A strip of cloth is forced between my teeth.

I fight harder. But there are too many hands. My mouth is gagged, and my wrists bound before me.

Dragged from the bed, I am set to my feet. Here I sway, disorientated, chest heaving, and feeling sick.

The shapes morph into people I do not recognize. Two are alphas, two more are betas.

Jessa, I see, is similarly gagged and bound. Our eyes meet, and I see my horror is reflected in the sweet young beta. Is this the Lyon clan? Have our warriors failed? I swallow thickly as fear for my mates overwrites fear for myself.

The tall, graceful woman who steps before me catches a shaft of light.

Nola.

My pounding heart rate elevates further. Nola's lips lift in a cruel smirk before she slaps me across the face.

The blow snaps my head to the side, and pain explodes across my cheek. The sounds of more scuffling and muttered curses follow.

"Leave off, bitch," a male voice says. "You can have your fun with her once we're out of Ralston."

Arm fisted by an alpha, I'm shoved roughly toward the window.

Distantly, I realize that Ralston has not fallen since they are thrusting us out through the window and not marching us down the front steps.

Wrists bound, and at Nola's insistence, Jessa and I are driven through the forest with a switch. The young beta is full of callous rage. I take small comfort that it's mostly I who must suffer Nola's spite. Every time Nola lands a blow upon Jessa, I swear I hear the Goddess weep. I am a small beta, but Jessa is even smaller and barely a woman.

Once clear of the village where we might raise the alarm, we are allowed to remove the gags. Without shoes, my feet are soon a source of fiery pain every bit as vicious as the welts left by the switch. It gets worse when I stumble on a rock, and a cut is opened. I know not where they take us. But the switch keeps us moving.

Soon, every step is like a knife stabbing in the sole of my foot. But Nola will suffer no delay.

We stop beside a river where more men and horses wait.

I sit. I cannot bear the pain in my right foot a moment longer. Jessa comes to my side, a little dirt mixed with the tears on her pretty face.

"Do you know these people?" I whisper.

She nods. "I recognize a warrior from the Lyon clan. Why Nola is with them, I do not know. I heard a man mention that you are to be bartered. The Lyon king's son has been taken, and they need you so that they might get him back."

"So you are here by association," I say. Pain has left me feeling queasy. But I am more wretched knowing that Jessa's presence in my home has led to her being caught up in this.

"Our warriors will come for us," she says, voice carrying quiet authority. "I wonder what has transpired for them to have captured Danon Lyon? It will not end well for them that they dared to take you as leverage." Her eyes glitter in the moonlight as she watches the group argue. "They will be well punished."

I can only pray that it is so.

Chapter Twenty-Four

Jack

I arrive at Halket as night is falling. Accompanying me is nearly fifty men: a combination of warriors from Ralston and two other clans. Tonight, I will take the war to the Lyons.

Only war has already arrived, and the bitter chaos calls.

Karry, the Halket king, is dead, and the clan is in a state of great sorrow and rage. Eric is a young alpha, but he must step up to the role for the sake of his people.

I find minor comfort in discovering that Fen has done me proud in his dealing with Eric.

The pyre to the late king burns bright in the night sky, and we gather around as the ashes rise to join the Goddess.

"Tomorrow," Eric says. "We will take the war to them. There can be no more diplomacy. The only words will be those delivered by the sharped steel of my sword."

I nod, but my gut is churning. I hate that I have left our mate unattended. "Tonight would be better," I say. I am bordering on disrespect with this comment while the late king is not yet fully gifted to the Goddess.

Eric turns to face me, and I see the indecision cross his face. Our two clans are closest together. The territory split where the river separates us and leads to the loch. The Lyon clan is northeast, half a day's ride away. "They came for your father," I say. "What else have they come for?"

I am thinking about Ralston, Hazel, and about our absence. Have we left them vulnerable? Warriors were left to guard, but now I suffer a sickness that tells me I should return home.

"Fuck! We have been away all day," Fen says. "We should question Danon."

"He is our prisoner," Eric says.

"We have left our fucking village vulnerable all day," Fen repeats, voice heating. "They killed your father. What's to say they have not attacked our home too?"

I see Eric's nostrils flare, and my temper rises. It's not only my temper, and I put a hand on Fen's shoulder, lest he does something foolish.

"We will question him again," Eric says. "The Goddess will understand. My father will understand." Turning, he calls two of his warriors.

But before we can seek to question Danon, horses thunder into the village.

They are Ralston warriors whom we left in the village. As the horses stop before me, a warrior calls the words I dread the most, "Hazel and Jessa have been taken!"

My lips tighten, and I clench my shaking fingers into fists.

My gaze shifts first to Fen before settling on Brandon, who is ever at Fen's side.

They have dared to take our women. Our retaliation will be swift and deadly for everyone involved.

Hazel

Mounted upon horses before Lyon warriors, we ride through the night. As dawn is creeping over the horizon, we arrive at their community. Nestled in the foothills of a mountain, it might have been a beautiful place in other circumstances. Now, it is a frenzy as women and wailing children flee. Villagers rush and run in every direction. Warriors bellow orders.

Chaos and bubbling dread hovers over the air.

As we pull up before a grand building, a great bear of an alpha emerges. An argument begins between those who took me and this new alpha.

"You are fucking stupid," I hear the bear-like alpha roar at one of the alphas who snatched us. "They will slit Danon's fucking throat that you took a bound mate from Jack and Fen. Snatch a couple of lower-ranking women, was my father's order. Not that I fucking agree with snatching a fucking lass. Nola is bitter that she was sent away as a slave. The beta is dishonored. She has led you all for fools."

I am all but tossed from the horse by the beta who held me, and my injured foot brings a cry to my lips.

Jessa hurries to support me as the arguing alphas draw a crowd.

"It is Danon's younger brother, Gage," she says softly.

Her voice, barely above a whisper, draws the giant male's gaze. His nostrils flare, and his fists clench as his gaze roams the length of the tiny beta standing at my side. The slightest gasp from Jessa and the tall, powerful alpha stares at us as we cling together, shaking. "What the fuck is the child doing here?"

"She was with their mate," Nola spits back. "And nothing short of their mate will have a chance to see your brother returned after what he has done."

So fast does Gage move that it is little more than a blur. Fist closing over the beta's throat, he lifts Nola clear off her feet. Her legs kick and thrash. Her fingers claw at the hands crushing her throat.

"I am not a child anymore," Jessa says.

Nola is dropped. Falling to the ground at the giant's feet, she gasps, fingers clutching her throat.

"Are you bonded?" Gage demands, closing in on us.

"No," Jessa says, body trembling beside mine even as she straightens her spine, drawing the beast's gaze to places it should not be. "Not yet. But I soon will be."

The alpha stalks closer toward us. Instinctively, I seek to back away, hissing as my injured foot contacts the floor. His dark gaze shifts my way. Jessa holds me tighter and tries to put her body before mine like it might save us from this brooding monster's wrath.

Gage stills, eyes shifting to Jessa. There is something between these two that I do not understand, yet I feel it all the same—a thick thread wrapping them up and drawing them tighter together.

"Kill the slave," Gage says, never taking his eyes from Jessa. "Snap her useless neck, slit her throat. I do not care."

The sounds of stammered pleading come from behind the great alpha. I want to beg for mercy for Nola, but my throat is dry, and no words come out. Nola's begging turns to screams and the screams to silence.

And still, Gage stares at Jessa.

"Well, this is a fuck up of unprecedented proportions. Between my father and my brother, it will be a wonder we have any clan left come the morrow." There is bitterness in his voice. And rage, there is also rage.

Finally, he drags his eyes from Jessa and directs his gaze at me. "Are you injured?"

I nod. I don't trust myself to speak—I don't think I can

speak. Gage has just ordered Nola's death. He has said our presence here is a disaster. Is he planning to kill us too?

"He won't hurt us," Jessa says, and despite the tension enfolding our patch of earth, I believe she speaks the truth.

Then the bear is upon us, and we are both picked up like we are naught but a couple of kittens. "Time to do what I should have done long since," he growls as he stalks past the larger home and out the back, bellowing orders to men.

"Where are you taking us?" Jessa demands. We both fight, although I cannot see it is doing either of us any good.

"Quieten down, lass. I am only taking you out of the way. There will be war here soon, and I would not have either of you hurt when lesser men get confused in their bloodlust."

Taken into a small outbuilding, we are placed in the corner. Here, Gage draws a dagger. Grasping Jessa's wrists, he cuts the binding before giving the blade to her.

A great roar goes up beyond the small wooden shack that raises the hairs on the back of my neck.

"Bar the door," Gage says, and pivoting, stalks out.

As he leaves, Jessa scrambles to her feet and slips the heavy bar into place. Hurrying back to me, she saws through the binding at my wrists.

"You seem to know him well," I say. "He did not seem as monstrous as I expected men of his clan to be."

She sits beside me, the knife held out in her hand, ready but trembling.

Outside the tiny shack, I hear the evidence of war in the shouts, cries, and screams.

"When I said I kissed a lad who was not Brandon," she says, the wistfulness back in her voice. "Gage was that lad."

Chapter Twenty-Five

Jack

My mind fluctuates between fear, rage, and savage self-reproach.

I have lost a mate once through illness. The prospect of losing another second chance through negligence is like a sickness festering in my soul. Where they have taken Hazel, I cannot know. Danon gives no answers in our limited time questioning him. There is little inclination toward mercy for the male who killed the Halket king. I believe he knows naught of his clan's plans to snatch our mate.

And Jessa, who we learned, had decided to keep Hazel company with us absent. Likely she was taken simply because she was there.

As we mount to leave, a Halket clan member informs Eric that Nola, the woman gifted to them as a slave, is missing. I want to discount it, to believe she has simply taken the opportunity to flee while the chaos ensues. But Nola is ever a twisted lass. I dedicated too much time to offering her respect she did not warrant. All in the hopes she would mature and step up to her role as a lead woman within the clan. Lesa warned me long ago to watch Nola.

Lesa, who never had a bit of suspicion or spite in her for anyone, cautioned me many times.

That I did not heed my late mate's warning is another canker, but this one in my heart.

If Nola is behind any of this, I will take pleasure in killing her myself.

The swirling ball of churning in my gut manifests into a battle rage as we approach the village of Lyon. The sky is lightened by the onset of dawn as we near. Prepared for our arrival, we meet patrols.

It does them no good, and we slay all we meet. If a few manage to escape to raise a warning, it matters not.

Let them prepare. Let them tremble in fear. I will destroy them all.

As we thunder into the village square, I leap from my horse. My ax cleaves the chest open on the first man who dares to challenge me. With Fen, Brandon, Glen, and other clans' support, we wreak destruction upon the Lyons.

Slashing, parrying, and battering, I use all my focus.

But as warriors fall under my savagery, I realize something is wrong. They fight with each other as much as they fight with us. What madness has consumed this clan?

"We need to fucking question them!" Fen roars at me as I kill another man.

I pause, blinking, chest sawing with harsh breath. I feel the trickle of my many enemies' blood rolling down my face.

"We need to find out where the fuck Hazel and Jessa are!" Fen says.

Fen, who is the one usually lost to the battle frenzy, is the one cautioning me in reason. The red haze seeps away, and I come back to myself.

Hazel. Jessa. We need to know where they are.

Around me lay broken bodies. The fighting has reduced to pockets. They are already well punished.

I swipe a hand down my face, sick to my gut because my mate is still lost.

"Fuck!" Brandon says. The lad is prolific with his cursing... and naked given he has shifted back to human form.

Then I see what has arrested his attention.

The Lyon King, Rendal, and his second son, Gage, fight.

A vicious, bloody fight.

A fight that I sense only one will survive.

Our continuing conflict with this clan balances on the outcome.

All other fighting has stopped. We are caught watching to see which way the final blade shall fall.

Blood splatters, blades ring, and fists fly amid snarls and growls of rage.

But the Goddess is watching this village deep in the eastern Hinterlands. With a roar so visceral it springs hairs on the back of my neck, Gage slays his father.

"Fuck!" Brandon snarls and there is a wealth of feeling behind that word. He and Gage have a history that I do not have time to fucking deal with now.

"Search the village!" I order. "Find our mates."

Hazel

Jessa and I cling together within the darkened shack as the sounds of battling grow louder and more frenzied.

"I do not think this is so safe?" I say to Jessa, who still holds Gage's blade out before her. There is only us in here, but I think it gives her comfort. I have found a sturdy plank of wood. Similarly, I take comfort in the weight of my weapon and will not hesitate to beat anyone who enters and tries to take us. We have been taken once. I will not allow us to be taken again.

The door rattles suddenly. We both cling tighter, respective weapons shaking in our hands.

A cracking crash follows as an ax slams into the door. A second blow disintegrates the wood, and the shattered door swings open.

I do not know the man standing there. He is not a Ralston warrior.

"Found them!" he calls. Lowering the ax, he stalks inside.

Jessa has not lowered her blade, so I tighten my fingers over the plank of wood and get ready to attack.

"I'm not going to hurt you," he says, eying the knife Jessa holds.

"He is Lyon," she hisses and lunges for him with the knife.

He laughs as he batters her strike away and fists her wrist. Crying out in pain, she drops the blade to the floor. Enraged, I put every bit of my strength into the blow as I send the great lump of wood crashing to the side of his head.

"Uff!" He grunts and releases Jessa just as I beat him over the head again.

He tries to snatch the wood from me, but I'm charged with wild fear, and I beat him once again. Jessa leaps for his back as he rips the wood from my hand. Roaring, he spins around as she sinks her teeth into his ear.

Snatching the blade from where it has fallen on the floor, I ready myself to strike.

Another great crash sounds behind me as the shattered door is slammed open

Jack!

The world turns to a jumble. Jessa is flung from the

warrior's back. Jack swings his arm, striking the Lyon warrior's head with his ax. It makes a sickening popping sound as it enters the skull and another as Jack yanks it back out. Blood arcs in a great spray. The warrior drops to his knees before crashing to the side, dead.

Eyes stretched so wide they hurt, I stare at the fallen man. I don't see Jack until his fingers gently enclose my hand. He coaxes the weapon from my fierce grip, and tossing it to the floor, heaves me into his arms, purring manically.

"Brandon," I hear Jessa sob. The fierce beta, soon to be mate, lifts Jessa into his arms.

"Fen," I say. "Where is Fen?"

"I am here, lass." As Fen presses up behind me, enclosing me between his body and Jack's, I feel myself go slack. I'm tingling everywhere and suddenly as weak as a newborn kitten.

"We've got you," Jack says. "You are safe now, our sweet little beta mate."

Jack

The feeling of her tiny, trembling body in my arms is enough to unman me. Tears run down my cheeks as the chill holding my chest a prisoner finally eases its grip.

I purr. I can hear Fen purring.

It makes no difference to our instincts that she is a beta.

She is ours, and she is safe. That is all I care about.

She is also fertile. Despite my prior belief in my self-control, the stress of the night and the fighting past has me hanging on by a thread.

"She is fertile," Fen says thickly. I hear my desperation for our mate echoed in his voice. "We need to get her home."

Hazel weeps and clings, insisting she inspect both of us

before she is satisfied that we are well. Not that I'm ready to put her fucking down.

"What is wrong?" I demand seeing her wince with pain. Instantly, I'm torn between checking what is troubling her and taking up my ax so that I might kill whoever was responsible.

"I cut my foot," she says. Growling low, I set her on the floor so I can see what has happened. It is not only her foot that has suffered. Her arms and legs are covered in welts.

"It was Nola," Jessa says.

Turning back, I see that Brandon has his soon-to-be mate in his arms.

"I will fucking kill her," Fen growls behind me. He will have to get in the fucking queue.

"She is dead," Jessa says. "Gage ordered her death for taking us."

I hear Brandon cursing; he would not appreciate the mention of the other male who is an alpha where he is a beta, nor what Gage's protectiveness toward Jessa implies.

Gage has a history with Jessa. One that tolerates no harm coming to the tiny beta.

A tic begins thumping in my jaw as I turn back to my little mate. I owe Gage for that. The alpha, who stood over his father's fallen body, was never cut from the same stone. He is a strong alpha where his father and brother were weak. Danon will not survive killing the Halket king. They will have fun with him before he dies.

It would seem the Halket clan is not alone in gaining a new king this day.

My lips tighten as I inspect Hazel's foot. It is filthy, and dirt has gotten into the wound. It is not deep, which is a small blessing, but it will need to be cleaned.

"I want to go home," Hazel says. "Please, I'm sore, but I just want to go home."

Ignoring her protests about going home, we cleanse it as best we can. Lifting her back into my arms, we emerge from the shack into a scene of devastation.

Gage still stands over the ruined body that was once his father. All around, more killing continues as Gage's supporters find and slay those who once supported his father. Collectively, the eastern clans have a bloody reputation. Today, that reputation is realized in all its devastating glory.

I try my best to keep Hazel's head in the crook of my neck, but her gasp tells me she is looking. "Close your eyes, lass," I say. "There is nothing here you need to see. We are going home now."

I meet Gage's steady gaze. He nods. We will need to talk soon. But not today.

Gage's eyes shift to the side, and I know he is staring at Jessa. I'd hoped that nonsense was long over and done with, but alas, an alpha is ever a determined beast when he sets his sights upon a mate.

A worry for another fucking time.

Now, Fen and I have a mate we need to care for.

Hazel

Jessa is carried by a naked Brandon, but I see her eyes dart to Gage as we emerge into the Lyon village. In my heart, I know there is unfinished business there.

I gasp as I take in the blood and death that has swept through the village.

Jack growls, cupping the back of my head against him as he stalks toward the horses. He tries to shield me from the terror, but it is too late, and I have seen. All around are the sounds of weeping, dying, and suffering. The Lyon clan has been well punished for what they dared to do.

"We ride!" Jack calls. Now the hoots of victorious warriors fill the air.

Tossing me up into the saddle, Jack mounts behind me. I swing my face around, making sure I can see Fen. He is behind us, mounting his horse, handsome face serious.

I know their tension is about more than my capture. I am fertile. Fen said as much, and they are compelled to rut me and get me with child.

The battle past has raised their blood lust. But there is only one place for such hunger to go.

Rutting.

Beta fertility has a rut-like impact upon an alpha. *"The scent of a fertile beta will rouse an increased appetite,"* Jack had said. *"Only unlike a rut, it is far more controlled, but no less compelling need to fill the sweet little beta all up."*

They are more controlled, for there are no pheromones at work. But as soon as we reach the safety of our home, they will need to couple with me. They will rut and knot me, over and over until I am bred.

And Goddess, I want them to. I crave the feel of them inside me, filling me all up. alphas are so basal compared to a beta male. They have rough ways and demands.

And a knot, they also have a knot. I am not frightened of it anymore. They have trained and prepared me.

My mates are fierce and protective. I loved them before the wicked lass, Nola stole me away. Now, I love my brave mates even more, and I wish to be perfect for them in every way.

Chapter Twenty-Six

Hazel

We ride for many hours. Exhausted by the terror of the events, I sleep fitfully.

The slowing of the horse rouses me, and I open my eyes to find we have arrived at the shores of the loch.

Ralston is a source of picturesque beauty in the glistening sun. The sky is bright and cloudless blue, while the trees covering the mountains' lower slopes are a vivid green. The loch barely suffers a ripple as it reflects the beauty of the scene. There is something about the closeness of death that makes my heart swell seeing the jumble of rooftops and buildings where the settlement meets the loch shore.

Home.

I have never thought of Ralston as my home. Now and today, I realize that this is where I shall live the rest of my life with my two proud mates. Here we will have children. We will watch them grow and have children of their own. With two such mates, I know we shall be safe. Villagers soon emerge, following us all the way to our home. Calling out for news of what has happened.

As we pull up the horses before the steps, Fen dismounts first. Gathering me from the horse, he carries me up the steps. I look back, seeing Jack addressing the assembling crowd. More returning warriors are dismounting, greeted by their loved ones.

"He will not be long," Fen says. "But they will be worried and need to hear what has happened. And they need to hear it from their king."

Food and drinks are set upon the table should we desire. Fen takes me straight to the furs where I am comforted by the familiarity and lingering scent. "Let's get this off," he says, stripping my tattered dress away and tossing it to the floor. He growls, eyes darkening as he skims gentle fingertips over the welts that litter my skin.

"May I enter?" Jessa and her mother wait at the bedding chamber door, arms laden with salves and clean bandages. Fen waves them in.

Shifted to wolf form, Brandon paces near the entrance, eyes never leaving Jessa.

"I am fine," I say. "You are injured, Jessa, too." She is as grubby and draggled as me and has clearly rushed to get supplies.

Tears dampen her cheeks as she kneels before me, placing the bowl and supplies beside her on the floor. "I am not hurt so badly. Only bruises for nothing broke the skin. Nola was determined to punish you. Bad enough what she did the first time," she says, voice low and angry.

Fen growl-purrs the whole time the two women tend to me. "My brave, sweet little beta," Fen says. "This will soon be over, and you will feel better." He holds me on his lap while they care for my wounds, purring and pressing kisses to my hair.

I am cleaned, each welt checked and treated as they work their way down my body.

Jessa's lips tremble when she gets to my injured foot. I wince and steel myself to be brave and endure the cleansing of the cut. They are gentle with me, but I still sob.

"They are too wicked," Jessa's mother says. "War is for warriors. To snatch lasses as are not warriors and treat them thus is sacrilege. The Goddess will not show them favor."

It stings, but less so as she applies the soothing balm and carefully bandages my foot. "You should not walk until it has a chance to heal," her mother says as she gathers the supplies before wrapping an arm around her daughter.

"That won't be a problem," Jack says from the entrance to the chamber. "Our mate will be busy for the next few days while we tend to her."

Dimples flash on Jessa's cheeks. Leaning in, she presses a gentle kiss to my forehead. "May the Goddess bless you with a child," she whispers before hastening out with her mother bobbing her head in deference to Jack.

Then Jack enters the bedding chamber, and my breath traps in my lungs as I study my fierce mate. Fen was my first kiss, but Jack was the first to show me pleasures. Individually, my two mates are stunning, but together they are beyond earthly dreams.

Jack growls as he strips. I have never heard him growl this way before. It is a terrifying sound. Yet, it is also the sound of my mate in great need, and I respond. Fen stands, laying me upon the bed with a gentleness that belies what will soon come.

Goddess, they are primal, deadly mates who have battled to keep me safe. I want to show them how well I love and need them. Eyes never leaving mine, they put aside weapons and strip their hide pants.

They are watching me in the way of an alpha who needs his mate.

My breath catches as all that this means crashes through my mind. Of all the times, this is the most important time for me to present. I feel better after I have been treated with care. The welts sting only a little. My foot is sore, but I barely notice it any more.

I need to present.

I *want* to present.

Laying back against the soft furs, my whole body softens, and I flush with anticipation. There is no fear in me; they have prepared me well for this day. The thought of them rutting me, of them filling me with their seed, of that seed catching inside me and blooming into life is more compelling than my next breath.

Gloriously naked, they approach the bed. Letting my eyes roam over their thick, brawny bodies until I arrive at their cocks. Thick, monstrous, and enough to make my mouth water, they hang heavy, bobbing. The tips glisten as copious pre-cum leaks. Unlike a beta male, there is a thick deep red swelling near the base—their knot.

I smile, and raising my knees, let my legs fall open and apart.

Their purrs shift to low growls. Fen fists his ruddy cock and slowly works his fist up and down.

Here, I lay, waiting, presenting myself to the dominant males that they may fully mate and breed me. "I am yours," I say. "I will take all of you tonight, or the Goddess may take me, for I would gladly die trying."

I see the softening in their faces before calculation takes its place.

"What a perfect little beta you are," Jack says. "You will not want for our attention. We will rut you through the rest of the day and the night if need be. We will take you over and over, one after another."

The thought of them taking me over and over makes me groan. "Please," I say. "Please, fill me." I am desperate for their touch, growing slick between my thighs in anticipation of the two powerful males making me completely theirs.

They do not move, and the air grows heavy with their rich scent.

Pheromones, Jack calls them. I am only a beta, and they do not have the same impact upon me. Although today, as they keep me waiting, I determine that I could not imagine more than this great deep, well of love and longing that courses through me.

Perfect, Jack said that I was perfect. But I think it is they who are perfect in every possible way.

They are both going to rut me. I know I will be sore long before they are done, but as Jack determined early on in our loving, I enjoy a little pain.

"Please," I say again. "I need you both. Please, take this emptiness away."

Fen

There is a feverish glisten to the face of the little beta open and waiting upon the bed. For a moment, I worry that it might be to do with her terrible suffering at Nola's hands. But as I open myself and my senses to Hazel, I understand her needs. She is fertile. The young, beautiful woman who presents so perfectly on the bed is waiting to be bred.

I want nothing more than to fall upon her, but I sense Jack has plans, and I do not want to interfere. My cock feels hot and unnaturally heavy in my hand. Soon, I am going to knot her. Once I knot her, there will be no going back. Thank fuck we have prepared her because her breeding scent is divine, and I know I will be a little rough.

A strange otherworldly sensation settles over me. I feel disconnected and hyperaware at the same time. My body is responding to our mate's need to be bred.

"I'm going into rut," I say, voice rough and scratchy in my throat. I know little of omegas, having only met a few who were mated and so muted to me. But I know omegas can handle an alpha rut when in heat, while a beta cannot.

"Aye," Jack says, voice holding the same edge. "A tempered version, heightened by the battle past, her changed scent, and her natural submission to us. Hazel will handle our needs. She is not averse to our rough ways, nor to a little pain with her pleasure."

He is right. Hazel will handle all we need.

I draw a deep breath. I can scent her weeping pussy, and I want to taste her.

But I want to rut her more.

Mesmerized by her presenting and the glistening slit of her pussy I don't even notice Jack move until his hairy ass blocks my view.

I growl. Jack throws a look over his shoulder and growls back. I want to fucking challenge him. I want to rip him away from the breeding beta and fill her first. His growl deepens. The sweet little beta spread out on the furs, whimpers.

Jack's growl dips to a purr, and he turns back to our mate.

Hazel

There is no preamble. No coaxing my body to respond. I am on fire, and the burning need will only be sated by my alphas. Jack leans over me. He has not cleaned and bears the scent of his alpha musk, smoke, and blood. I try to grab his cock that I might bring it closer to where it needs to be. Jack is having none of it. He takes my wrists in a single giant hand, and with a sharp growl, pins them to the bed above my head.

"Our mate is out to test us," Jack drawls. Out the corner of my eye, I see Fen move to the side of us. It makes me even hotter seeing both of them watching me like this and seeing my neediness. I force my legs to open wider still and push my breasts out.

Jack's grin is all teeth. But I do not linger on his face for long as my eyes lower to his thick, jutting cock. It appears even bigger, hanging heavily between my splayed thighs. It leaks a thin, sticky trail of pre-cum all the way to the furs. Goddess, help me. Alpha males are so basal. I try to lift my hips, placing them closer to his huge cock.

His other hand splays over my abdomen, pinning me against the bed. "Be still," he growls. "You will get plenty of attention tonight, my sweet little beta."

Taking his cock in hand, he lines up with my slick pussy and thrusts.

My back arches and I groan at the glorious fullness as he seats all the way in. "Goddess, yes!"

"Good girl," he says, voice a low rumble. "All filled up. Does that feel better?"

"Yes!" He is not moving. He should be moving, and I strain under his bulk, clenching over this thick rod buried inside me, trying to entice him to rut. "Please!"

"Gods, she is impatient," Fen says, a note of wonder in his voice. "Are you all the way inside?"

"I am," Jack rumbles. "And it feels fucking good. I will not last long. The little brat is clenching something fierce." I see his eyes darken with feral intent. "But she will soon repent her naughtiness when I begin to work my knot in and out."

Releasing my wrists, he takes hold of my waist, rises, and

slams me off and on his length.

I squeal as nerves the length of my channel rush to life.

"Goddess!" A shiver ripples through me as the knot slips out and then in. "Oh!!!"

Then he does it again, and again, and I climb toward the blissful high swiftly.

He purr-growls as he ruts me. I rake the furs beneath me, trying to find a source of stability in this storm. I am so full inside, all tingly and throbbing and glorious at the same time. The rippling sensation of his knot is making me absolutely wild. The fullness every time it enters me, is like a spiral pulling me ever tighter and higher.

"Fuck," I distantly hear Fen say. "Fuck, she is taking your knot so well."

The furs dip as Fen lays beside me. Taking my hand, he places it over his cock, groaning as I begin to pump up and down the thick shaft. Cupping my cheek, he turns my face toward his. Eyes darkening, he drinks in my tormented pleasure. "Such a good girl," he says before forcing three fingers deep into my mouth.

I gag, my pussy clenches. "Mmnnn!"

"Oh fuck, she really liked that," Fen says. Removing his fingers, he closes his lips over mine and pinches over my nipple hard before rolling it roughly. I groan into his mouth as our tongues meet and tangle. My hand pumps erratically over his weeping cock. He thrusts into my fingers and deepens the kiss.

There are too many sensations at once, and all of them are divine. But the feeling of Jack's cock slamming in and out of my pussy builds a primitive kind of urgency. I wrench my lips from Fen's, sucking air into my lungs. My eyes lower, and a deep groan rises from my chest. The knot is obscenely swollen, thick, round, and purple. I groan again, wanting to tear my eyes away and yet mesmerized. My jaw hangs slack, my pussy strains to accept the monstrous knot. I am so slippery; I'm sure that is the only reason it can breach me at all.

Jack's hands tighten on my waist. He growls. He can barely force it in. Fen squeezes and tugs my nipple cruelly as he nuzzles the side of my throat.

"Oh! Goddess! Please! It won't fit."

Then it slips inside in a rush. "Ohgodohgodohgod!"

Jack

She is coming. The sensation of her pussy milking my knot is sublime. My balls tighten, and jet after jet of hot cum spews out. Fen palms her throat, holding our writhing mate still. "Good girl, such a good girl," he croons. "That feels so good, doesn't it? We are going to fill you up so well."

Back arching against the furs, she is either trying to buck me off or pull me in, it is hard to tell.

I pin her tighter to me and jet more cum into her womb.

"You will not leave these furs until you are good and bred," I say, rocking my hips against hers because it feels so fucking amazing when it makes her squeeze over my knot. "Your hot little cunt has taken all my cock and knot."

She groans, half insensible with her climax. I smirk contented to the depth of my soul as my cock jerks through the after-shocks.

Fen kisses her cheek and down her throat, sucking little bites while humping into her grasping hand. "Fuck, I need to rut her. I am going to fucking come if I don't get inside her soon," he mutters between kisses.

He can wait. I am first among us, and my seed will be planted first. I keep jetting more, my balls tightening to the point of pain as they reach for every drop of seed.

I am calm again now that I have filled my sweet little beta

all up. Were it not for Fen growing ever more restless, I would tuck the lass under me until my knot properly softened.

But there is not only me. There is another mate who has needs. So the moment my knot softens enough, I steel myself and pull out.

"Oh!"

"Hush," I say, gathering her hands when she tries to cover her gushing pussy up. "Let me see."

"No!"

She gets a smack to her thigh when she tries to close her legs.

"Gods," Fen says, a note of wonder in his voice. He leans up, and like me, is riveted by the sight of her ruined pussy leaking out my cum.

I want to fucking plug her again as I see the cum trickling out, saturating her all the way to the furs. I push a couple of fingers in, growling as I feel how open she is.

"Fuck," Fen mutters. His need to rut is momentarily forgotten as he pushes a finger in roughly beside mine.

"Goddess, please!" Hazel wails.

Fen smirks and thrusts a second finger in. "Pull her open," he says. "I want to see."

With our fingers speared deep inside her, we gently pull her open, and another great gush of cum pours out. I rest my palm over her tummy and gently push, ejecting yet more cum.

Filthy and intensely arousing all at once, my dick jerks in anticipation of filling her all up again. But I must wait my turn, for Fen rolls above her and rams his cock deep.

Hazel

I don't like the feeling after Jack pulled his knot out. My poor pussy was so open and achy before they tried to stretch me even more.

But this thrusting fullness as Fen pounds into me—this I like.

My body rises. It's like I am sitting on the edge of bliss, teetering permanently on the slimmest thread.

Above me, Fen's handsome face has taken on a savage edge. He uses me roughly, not hesitating to work his growing knot in and out. My newly stretched muscles are sore in the best kind of way.

"Harder," I say. Then want to swallow my stupid tongue for making such a request. But I am so close to the sharp bliss that will consume me when I come, and a little more will get me there.

Fen's face darkens, taking on a sinister gleam as he rips out. "Oh!"

What? Why?

I am tossed over onto my belly. Fen's big hands circle my waist, dragging my ass up and back.

"Mmnnn!" I moan into the furs as Fen fills me once again. This position allows him to go even deeper, and I'm soon gasping and trying to wriggle away when he batters that sensitive place deep inside.

"Good girl," Jack says. He gathers my wrists, pinning them to the bed before my face so that I cannot get enough leverage to struggle. "We need to take you extra deeply so that our seed can fully fill you. Try and relax and let Fen take you how he needs."

I wail out my protest, trying not to listen to the filthy wet sounds it makes as Fen fucks me deep and fast.

"Oh! He is swelling!"

Jack toys with my hair, watching my tormented face as Fen begins to slow, forcing the knot in and out. I try to fight it, but my poor pussy has no choice but to give.

"Fuck, fuck, fuck," Fen growls behind me. "I am knotting her. I'm knotting her, our sweet beta mate." He pulls his knot out one last time before tightening his hold on my waist and battling to stuff it back in.

I wail, screech, and thrash as the thick swelling is forced all the way in where it nestles, plugging me. Then my pussy convulses around the knot. Dark and twisty pleasure and pain merge with blinding lights as my pussy clenches. I hump myself back so that I might get more. Hot gushes pulse inside me as he gently rocks his hips growling and purring his pleasure.

"She fucking loves a knot," Fen says roughly.

So much cum is filling me. It drips and trickles down my thighs and onto the soft furs.

"Oh! My tummy hurts!" He does not seem to stop coming, and a terrible pressure builds deep inside me as the knot holds everything inside.

"You will need to get used to this," Jack says. "Try and bear it for a little longer."

I don't have a choice.

"Clench," Fen demands.

"No!"

I hear his dark chuckle as his fingers find my swollen clit. He begins to strum it roughly, and my pussy immediately tightens.

"Good girl," Jack says. "Best you learn to do as you're told." My body is in flames when Jack captures my sore nipple and tugs and pinches it roughly.

I shatter. The climax is even darker and more twisted than the last one. It gathers up every part of me, washing over my skin, blazing in a golden line between my nipple, clit, and stuffed pussy.

I twitch and moan against the furs, belly and pussy aching with the strain.

The relief when Fen pulls the knot out is profound. The moment they release me, I press my fingers to my swollen tummy.

"I need to rut her again," Jack says. He shifts, and I groan weakly. I'm not sure I can take more.

"She is all full up," Fen says. "She is wasting a lot."

"That can't be helped," Jack says. Reaching under me, he brushes my hands aside and closes his big hand over my tummy. He pumps it just as he thrusts his fingers in and out of my pussy.

"Oh! What are you doing?" I find hidden reserves of energy under this savage pumping. Wet splashing noises follow as all the cum they have pushed into me is forced back out.

"Fuck," Fen says gruffly when Jack finally stops. "I don't think I can wait my turn."

I am utterly limp against the bed in the aftermath. But the terrible pressure has gone.

"Best you use her pretty mouth while I fill her up again." Grasping my hips, he feeds his cock into my pussy.

I groan. I am so slick and open and fluttering in eagerness for the next rutting.

"Open up," Fen says, tipping my face to the side and presenting me with his weeping cock. Dutifully, I open, and he surges deeply.

I groan around the hot flesh filling my mouth as Jack fills my pussy.

Here, right here, I know what it is to be alive.

Under their skilled attention, I climb over and over to rapturous heights. I forget about the terrors of the day and night past. Instead, I lose myself in the loving, wicked attention of my mates.

Chapter Twenty-Seven

Hazel

"Uh!" I push the cup away, only for Jessa to push it back.

"Mama says it is good for you and the babe," she says, smirking.

"You are jesting with me," I say, trying and failing to determine the truth.

"Go on, lass," her mother says, bustling into the cottage that Jessa still shares with her parents and five other siblings. Her mother is a plain-talking woman with a little grey at her temples and dimples when she smiles. I see a lot of her reflected in her daughter except her eyes, for they come from her papa. She carries an armful of washing, which she sets on the table and begins to fold. "I would not joke about such matters. It smells foul for sure. But it's full of healthy things that benefit a lass with child. The Baxter clan king has an omega mate, who has great skill in herbal teas, among other things. And you have two such hale mates, I can only presume that it must be an alpha babe. You will surely need all the help you can get! Give it another spoon of honey, Jessa."

Jessa rolls her eyes but spoons another dollop of honey in before placing it before me. "There," she says. "Don't be a wuss about it."

Before I can pick it up, a great wail comes from the open door as Jessa's youngest sister, Greta, toddles into the cottage bemoaning how her brother has stolen her favorite stick.

Jessa scoops the noisy brat up and puts her on her lap. "There now," Jessa says. "We shall get you another stick. But first, we need to make sure Hazel drinks the tea that Mama made for her."

Greta's eyes go wide; the tears stop as she peeks at me from under dampened lashes.

"She is being very naughty about it," Jessa continues. "And we know what happens when a lass is naughty about drinking Mama's healing tea."

"She gets a spanking and dry bread for supper!" Greta announces gleefully, like I have already failed in this task.

The stick is forgotten amid my misfortune, it would seem.

"Go on," says Jessa's mama, shaking her head. "Not one of you has ever gotten a spanking for not drinking tea! Such fibs you all tell."

Greta giggles and sing-songs, "Hazel is getting a spanking!"

I cut a glare at Jessa, although I'm also fighting a smile. Making a show of pulling a face, I draw the cup to my lips.

Greta cackles as I gulp the hideous concoction down. When I'm done, Greta demands to see the cup that she might be sure I drank it all. "There is some left!" she announces, although there is no more than dregs.

Pulling another face that is not all for show, I drink the last part up. "Uh!" The last dregs were dreadful.

"Hail! What are you all doing inside when there is a fire and feasting to be had?" The gruff beta male who enters the cottage is Jessa's papa. He is surrounded by the other children who all burst into the home amid great excitement, whooping and squealing. Their father rolls his eyes at their ruckus. Patting his wife's ass, he plants a kiss on her cheek.

The kids all make exaggerating kissing noises. "Bloody brats!" he says. Turning, he issues a fake monster growl and chases them back out of the house.

"Eh, they will never sleep tonight," Jessa's mother says, laughing.

I'm laughing too as I thank them for the tea and take my leave with promises to see them at the feast.

As I walk the narrow village path to my home, I feel a giddiness in my step. When I was a young lass, I could not have dreamed of finding myself so happy. Two amazing mates and a babe growing in my belly. My home is a beautiful place, and the warm, caring families like Jessa's make it even better.

Arriving at the steps of our home, I see Fen talking to Brandon. The light has begun to fade, and lanterns have been lit. Fen is so handsome; it hardly seems possible that the young alpha who stole my first kiss should come to be my mate all these years later.

He turns on hearing my approach, and whatever Brandon is saying is forgotten as Fen smiles at me. My tummy does that little tumbling thing. This is love, I realize, this warm feeling that grows in my belly and in my chest whenever one of my mates turns my way, smiles, or holds me—a beautiful sensation of being home that is about more than a place.

"I'll see you at the feast," Fen says to Brandon, never taking his eyes from me. Smirking, Brandon stalks off. As I near, a strange shyness settles over me. Fen snakes an arm around my waist as I try to dart past, pinning my back flush to his chest. "Where do you think you're going?" he demands. Lowering his lips to my throat, he nibbles up the side in a way that makes me squirmy.

"I need to get ready!"

"I need to rut you," he growls, hand lowering until it rests over my belly. "I can't wait for this to get bigger." His hands slide to cup my breasts. "And these."

"What are you two up to?" Jack demands, approaching from inside the home. His expression is very stern, and his eyes lower to where Fen is cupping my breasts. "There is a feast, and we need to be there."

"I need to rut her," Fen says.

I bite my lower lip when Jack's nostrils flare. I swear they set each other off when it comes to rutting. It has been a few weeks since the fateful night when Jessa and I were taken captive. Since then, they have been attentive to bedding me in the furs, and elsewhere. They take turns to feed me breakfast and supper. An event that as often as not leads to them making me feel good before a swift rutting.

I admit I encourage them. Jack says it is my pregnancy at work. But I think it is just the natural impact of a lass having the constant attention of two such virile mates.

"She wants it," Fen says confidently when Jack does not move. His hands lower to my waist again. I'm a little disappointed.

Jack's face softens, and his hooded gazed lowers to meet mine. "The lass is naturally lusty," he says, stepping into me, crowding my small body back into Fen. Goddess, it makes me hot and breathless when I am pinned between their strong bodies like this. "We will tend to her tonight before the stars and Goddess," he adds decisively. "Once the children have been sent to bed. We have not yet taken her thus and before the clan."

Heat fills my cheeks. I have heard whispered conversations about feasts. Jessa is excited. This is the first time she will not be sent home with the children. It is the first time she may be with Brandon as a woman is with a man, if she chooses to. I have a feeling that she might decide to make Brandon wait.

Then there is the unfinished business between Jessa and Gage, who, by all accounts, is bloodthirsty and ruthless.

But that is another story that is yet to unfold.

"Tonight then," Fen says, and stepping back, lands a firm swat on my ass. "Best get yourself ready, lass."

Jack

We both watch our sweet little mate run inside to wash and change with a smile on our faces. Not so long ago, I had forgotten how to smile. There was little happiness in my life. I was existing, but not living.

"She has been good for you," Fen says, catching me staring into the house like the love-sick whelp that I am. I ought to cuff my insolent brother for making light of what was a difficult time of my life. But I don't. He means well.

He is also right.

"She has been good for both of us," I counter. Fen is not so young, but he has never matured until he needed to step up and assume his duties toward the clan. A change that only happened since he took Hazel as a mate. She has matured him, just as she has softened the pain that once held me. We laugh a lot now. We also spend a great deal of time loving her in the furs, and wherever else we catch the little imp and can engage in a swift rutting.

"Aye," he agrees, grinning.

Hazel

A great fire blazes on the shore of the loch. The clan gathers around on the grassy banks. Here, they spread out blankets and furs. Lanterns hang from tall poles thrust into the ground giving the feast a magical feel. Food and drinks are brought out: Roasted pork, salmon, trout, duck, and honeyed wine and beer. There is music and dancing. Children and adults alike are full of merriment. Tonight, Jack is the one who feeds me as I sit on his lap. Fen chats to a young warrior, but his eyes often stray toward me.

As the sun sets fully and darkness takes the lands, the children are sent to their homes under the watch of older siblings, and those not inclined toward the Goddess worshipping that happens after dark.

The music picks up a different kind of beat, one that I feel all the way deep inside. I am given over to sit on Fen's lap, where I am lulled by the music. He presses kisses to my fingers, arms, and throat. Heat is building inside me, slow and languid.

The Goddess is here. I can feel her presence. Her voice and love are carried on the cooling breeze and dance across the still waters of the loch. It seems entirely natural when Fen slips a hand under the hem of my skirt and trails his fingertips over the tops of my thighs. Soon, I'm needy for them to reach other places.

Fidgeting, I try to move the situation to my liking. Fen laughs, low and husky against my ear. "Our mate is getting needy," he says.

My eyes shift to where Jack lounges close by, watching us

with the same hunger I feel in my belly—one that is nothing to do with food. I don't look, but I can hear rutting: the soft moans, the slaps of flesh. It merges with the beat of the music, slipping under my skin, making me hot and desperate.

I bite my lower lip, and, meeting Jack's eyes, let my legs fall open.

His answer is a growl as he grasps my ankle, spilling me backward onto Fen. Dress thrust up, he buries his head between and eats my pussy with noisy enthusiasm that has me panting and gasping.

Fen tugs my dress up and off. His big hands cup my breasts, squeezing them together before tugging on my nipples. "Good girl," he says. "Let yourself come."

My chest stutters. The sensation of Jack's tongue, lips, and teeth moving all over my pussy has me tingling and feverish with need.

"Let yourself come," Fen coaxes. "Then we will fill you all up just how you like and need."

The heat rises inside me, higher. I twitch and strain, but they tighten their hands on me to still me and continue the sweet torment. A low gasping moan rolls through me with the climax that is so blissfully sweet and deep, it sends me spinning.

My chest heaves in the aftermath. Jack lifts his head, smirking. I twitch when he runs a thick finger down between my pussy lips and gently presses it inside. "Goddess!"

"Hands and knees," Fen says, lips beside my ear. My pussy clenches over Jack's fingers. All his attention has done is make me desperate for more.

There is no hesitation. I want him to rut me. I want them both to rut me before the Goddess so that she might know how well the mates she has chosen for me love me and I them.

Jack chuckles at my eagerness. But then Fen fills me with his cock, and all three of us groan.

Fen

We take turns rutting our sweet mate. The lass is lusty with her pregnancy. It is for the best there are two of us; she would surely wear either one of us out. We have both enjoyed her pussy, and now Jack is enjoying her pretty mouth.

She still does not take as well to cock sucking as either of us might prefer. There is a lot of fuss if we try to go too deeply... Then there is her inclination toward spitting the cum back out.

Usually, I am well sated and only find it amusing. But alas, Jack sees it as the gravest of insults, which I also find amusing.

Tonight, as Jack comes in her mouth, I sense that Hazel is not going to be good about swallowing it.

"Do not fucking spit it out," Jack says, a glint of determination in his eye that suggests she's about to get her bottom spanked if she defies him.

I grin.

She shakes her head and starts to turn away.

I chortle. Hazel does not like swallowing but especially if there is a lot.

"Don't—" Jack warns. Too late as he pinches her cheeks, it all spews out.

"Oops," she says.

My laugh turns to a deeper guffaw.

"Little brat," Jack says, shaking his head at the mess Hazel has made. He swipes his thumb over her chin. There is not a lot there, but he is making a point.

She opens dutifully. But no sooner does Jack press his thumb into her mouth than he is pulling it back out again with a growl.

"Did she bite you?" I venture to ask, holding my stomach, which is aching from my laughter.

Smugness flashes in her eyes until Jack scoops her off the floor. Her squeal is cute and ripe with fake outrage.

"Best we take the lass to the furs," Jack calls over his shoulder. "Her training is nowhere near complete!"

Chapter Twenty-Eight

Hazel

I spend the morning with an omega from the Baxter clan. She is an older lady, long past her breeding age with a kindly disposition and a great bear of a mate. Having never met an omega before, I am in awe of the tiny woman with a beguiling way. It seems she regularly visits adjoining clans in alliance with Baxter and offers advice to young betas mated with an alpha. More often, an alpha mates with more than one lass. So I am in an unusual situation.

We meet in the herb cottage, as it is known, where the clan stores all the healing herbs and roots. Her mate looms in the door as she sets about making tea from the supplies.

"You are fortunate, Hazel," she says. "In being mated to two such strong alphas. Many alpha mates do not know how to temper their natural way as they train a beta for their pleasure."

Her great mate mutters about 'women's talk' before he stomps off down the steps.

"All alphas have a high appetite for rutting," she says, smiling as she passes me the tea. "This will help. I will give you the recipe before I leave."

My face flames as I take the cup with my thanks and a nod. We take a seat and talk. I'm delighted by the insights, which help me to better understand the ways of an alpha. I cannot change what I am any more than my mates can change what they are. But like all things in life, if we learn about each other, we can find ways to meet in the middle.

"Do they show interest in a nest?" she asks. "Have they offered you the softest pelts for your bedding area?"

"They have," I confess. I had realized that they are enamored with the thickness and softness of pelts and furs supplied for the bed. Suspecting that they drew similarities between it and a nest.

"It has a calming influence on an alpha. An omega needs a nest to feel safe, and for nurturing when she is with child. An alpha is very respectful of a nest. Such behavior is instinctual to them. Whether you are an omega makes no difference to their need to keep you safe. Your mates will be deeply troubled that you were snatched. Building a nest in your bedding area will help to temper their high aggression after the event. Even though nesting is not natural to a beta, there are basic principles to the design that are easy to follow." She smiles kindly, pausing to refill my teacup. "I know many betas who settle with their alpha, come to love the nest and the purr."

"Oh, I love their purr already," I assure her.

She pats my hand. "There, I could tell that you would. I have a feeling you may be the first mate to bear an omega child in many generations. It is much more common if there are two alpha mates. If that happens, we will need to talk again." Her smile is knowing, like there might be secret things involved should I become a mother of an omega child.

I am both excited and nervous about all this.

We spend a bit of time discussing the local herbs and how to make the tea. Molly assures me that they will help keep me in the best health for both my mates' vigorous needs and the growing babe.

A babe. How I wished with all my heart to be gotten with child, and how happy I am that it has happened.

Our time ends when Molly must offer advice to another beta. "The poor lass is mated to an alpha who does not possess either the wits or skills of your Jack and Fen," Molly says. "But she loves him dearly, and he, her, so I do what I can to help guide her."

Leaving the herb cottage, I enlist the assistance of Jessa, and we set about creating a nest.

"Omegas are an odd lot," Jessa says as we enter my bedding chamber, arms laden. "I mean, building a nest, like an animal might. That is a strange set of affairs."

Chuckling, I put my bundle of furs beside the bed. "I am with child now. And after everything that has happened, I want to please them." There was a time when I thought the Goddess had abandoned me. But then she sent Jack and Fen, and I know it was a test to ensure they were worthy mates. Now I too must be worthy. Often, Jack or Fen get that glint in their eyes and talk about how well they have bred me. My hand strays to my tummy. I cannot wait to meet him or her. "Molly suggested that a nest would present well. I would do anything for my mates."

Jessa smiles kindly. "I would do anything for Brandon, and he for me. So although this is strange, I understand why you would do it." She dumps her pile of furs beside mine.

An omega nesting is a private thing. They do not allow anyone else to be involved, not even their mates. But I am a beta, and I find I appreciate another's insight. Besides, Jessa has become a dear friend to me.

"How do we do this?" she asks.

"We have to make an edge by folding the pelts over." Selecting a pelt, I show her what I mean. Jessa busies herself folding the pelts for me, and I begin putting them in place at the edges of the bed. "Molly said that it would make them respectful of my space," I say, thinking about my mates' propensity for tossing the furs everywhere. "And they are not respectful now."

"No male is respectful of a woman's bed," Jessa says, giggling. "All they think about is rutting." Her smile is sly. "But I don't mind the rutting so much." She blushes prettily. "I like it quite a lot."

I laugh at her blush even as I am blushing myself.

She sends me a conspiring glance. "You do not mind them rutting so much yourself either if the sounds that come from this house are anything to go by."

"I also do not mind the rutting," I admit.

We both laugh.

It takes us a good while before I'm satisfied with the nest. As I stand back, we both agree that it is both strange and compelling.

"I like it," Jessa says. "It looks warm and snuggly." She taps her chin and sends a glance my way, along with an impish grin. "But I still think your huge males will destroy it when they try and climb in. Maybe we should put some pelts on the floor and encourage them to sleep there?"

We both laugh again. The image of my alphas sleeping on the floor when their mate is in bed is ridiculous.

A call comes from beyond the screen for Jessa.

"I better go," she says, smirking. "Enjoy your new nest."

Winking, she darts out.

. . .

The nest *is* too inviting, and I elect to take a nap. The babe is not yet enough to even show, but my mates insist that I take an afternoon nap since they often keep me awake with their attention of a night.

It feels strange as I slide into the nest. Warm and snuggly, as Jessa said, it encloses me on all sides and above. But as I lay there, my thoughts turn to consider how my mates might react to finding me here.

I grow restless and needy in the nest as I imagine them taking me together.

What will they do if they return and find my bottom oiled and plugged?

A small groan escapes my lips as I imagine their reaction. I have never done it myself before. Now, I cannot possibly rest for I am thinking about the plug and the wriggling stretching feeling as it goes in...and the way it makes my pussy grow slick.

Lifting my head from under the covers, I listen for sounds. It is still early. I can still do this before they return. I don't like the thought of being caught in the act, but I like the idea of them finding me prepared.

On the table beside the bed is the small box where all the plugs and phallus are placed against a fur lining after cleansing. A little bottle of natural oil is also there.

Feeling both naughty and wanton, I lift the lid on the box. It is only after I have the oil and the smallest plug in my hands that I realize this is not so easy to do to yourself. But I am determined, and I feel extra naughty as I carefully coat the plug with a little oil...and push.

It pops in with only a little discomfort. The plug I have selected does not go deep, but it holds me open. I groan a little as I put the oil back and snap the lid closed.

My intention is only to rest, but I'm soon asleep...

A warm, calloused hand soothing over my ankle, wakes me with a start. I bite back a groan when it makes me clench over the little plug. "Oh!" My ankle must have poked out of a pelt as I slept, and I snatch it back inside. I hear the purring, the one I recognize as Jack, and my thudding heart rate slows.

"May I enter the nest with you, my sweet little beta?" he asks.

"There is not enough space," I say, biting my lip to smother my laugh. Normally, Jack would blunder into the bed, snatch me up, and ready me to take his cock. Today he is respectful and *tentative*.

His hand slides under the covers. Capturing my ankle again, he rubs circles that feel nice. My plugged bottom keeps clenching, and my pussy is absolutely drenched.

"I will fit," he says. "I will be gentle about it. I will hardly disturb it at all. You are with child and must have your mates with you to feel properly safe, even in the nest."

Nest. He has never called it a nest before.

I smirk at this strange sweetness in my dominant mate. "Okay, if you are very gentle."

He is not gentle. I hear clothing and boots being tossed aside. Then he enters the nest. It is like an ox shouldering his way in and threatening to destroy the nest in his haste. His purr turns utterly manic. As soon as Jack has squeezed his way in, he palms my breast and begins nuzzling my throat. I am primed and ready for his attention, and I push my chest out, offering him better access.

"Does my sweet little mate need her pussy tending to? I think you might rest better after you have been well rutted and are thoroughly scented."

My stomach does that little dip-clench thing. I'm not averse to any of this suggestion. I have prepared myself for such.

At the sound of approaching footsteps, we both still.

"I need to come in," Fen says. The sounds of clothing being stripped, follows. Jack chooses that moment to enclose my nipple in his hot mouth.

"I don't think there is room," I say on a moan. Jack's purr increases halfway to a growl, and I curl my fingers in his hair. Beyond the pelts, I can hear Fen's purr.

"I will be fucking careful," Fen says. "But I need to come in, and I need to tend to you too!"

Jack closes his teeth around my nipple. A sharp little bite accompanies him easing two thick fingers into my slick pussy. "What a naughty, wet little pussy," Jack growls. "Has my mate been thinking naughty thoughts?" The lingering sting on my nipple is so good, and I try to ride his fingers.

"I am still fucking waiting!" Fen growls. I feel wicked for forgetting he was there.

"Okay," I say, gasping as Jack sucks hard on my sore nipple and swipes his thick thumb over my clit. My bottom is clenching in excitement. I am half-wild with my needs.

The nest nearly collapses as Fen forces his way inside. Spooning behind me, his lips seek my throat. My legs are parted, my thigh lifted open over Fen's. His finger plunges in beside Jack's, and they both finger fuck me. Jack growls. Fen growls back, and my stupid body gushes around their fingers.

"She is very fucking tight," Fen says. I groan, fearing he has realized what I have done.

Their growling settles to a purr. Thick fingers clashing as they thrust in and out.

Then they begin pulling, gently *stretching* me open ready for their pleasure.

"Our mate has great needs tonight," Jack says. "She will need to be well rutted so that she feels safe."

"We will fill her together," Fen says. "That is her favorite way when she is thoroughly rutted between us."

Then Fen slides his fingers back, and his purr lowers to a growl. "Goddess," he says as his fingers brush the handle of the plug. "She has oiled and plugged her bottom." He catches the handle, turning it, pulling it almost out, and thrusting it back again.

"I need to see," Jack says. I am rolled onto my tummy, the nest imploding as they part my legs and gently open the cheeks of my bottom so they can better see what I have done.

"She is perfectly trained," Jack says thickly. I whimper as their fingers pet and play with the little plug. "No wonder her pussy is so slick and ready. Have you taken your afternoon nap plugged thus?"

"Yes," I say. "After I made the nest, I was feeling naughty." I groan as the handle is grasped to tease it in and out. The stretching sensation as it comes all the way out and pushes all the way back in has me gasping and groaning. Then it disappears altogether, and thick fingers take its place.

"All oiled and slick," Fen says. "She is nicely open. There will only be a pleasurable amount of discomfort as I thrust my cock deep in here."

"Our sweet little beta mate has prepared herself to be ravished," Jack says. "She has made a nest for us to rut her in."

"We will soon destroy this nest as we fuck her," Fen says, thick fingers sliding in and out of my ass before circling the little entrance and filling me again.

"You are not supposed to ruin the nest!" I say on a whiny groan. "An alpha should respect the nest."

"Whoever told you that nonsense," Jack says, grasping my chin, he tilts my face from the furs so he can see my face. He is wearing a wicked kind of smirk. "An alpha loves nothing better than ruining a nest as he ruts his mate. But we will help you put it back together when we are done. Now, do you need your mates to rut you? Do you need us both to fill you together?"

"Yes," I say. "Please, I need you both together."

"Goddess, she is perfect for us," Fen says.

"She is," Jack agrees. "Our perfect little mate. She is well trained for our pleasure. Our pleasure, and hers."

Epilogue

Hazel

It takes us a whole day to reach the town of Oxenford. Leaving at first light and arriving as the sun is setting. Word was sent to Papa a couple of weeks ago to let him know.

We will spend a little time here so that my father might meet his granddaughter. Afterward, we will travel the greater distance to the lordly residence where my mates' sister lives. A carriage is being sent to offer comfort to the babe and me. I tried protesting that a cart would be plenty good enough, but neither of my mates will hear a word of it. Secretly, I admit to being much enamored with traveling in comfort. I'm also excited to meet their sister, if a little nervous about her being bound to a fancy lordling. Both Jack and Fen speak with affection for their sister, and I already know that I will love her.

There is also a note of pride in my mates, for they are both besotted with our little girl. I know they cannot wait to introduce little Mia to her aunty and uncle.

261

When I left Oxenford, my friends and acquaintances watched with wary eyes as the barbarian king stole me away. But today, as we ride down the high street, they gather at doors and pause work that they might wave. Where once they looked upon me with pity, now there is acceptance. Some finish tasks before hastening to join us. Others shout promises to visit with me later or on the morrow that they might meet my babe.

My father, a gruff man, has a tear in his eyes as he steps out of his workshop to greet us. Here, outside the little cottage where I grew up, a place once full of laughter and love, and even sadness as is the natural part of life, my papa gets his first cuddle with my babe.

"She has your eyes," he says, stroking a rough finger used to holding a hammer gently over Mia's soft baby cheek. "She has your mother's eyes," he adds softly. "Ah, she was an angel, Goddess rest her soul. What did you call the babe?" he asks.

There is something about seeing the tiny wriggling bundle in the rough farrier's arms, and seeing the gentle care and loving in his eyes that brings a sense of completion. There was a time when he held another babe, his first daughter. I imagine him holding her with similar wonder and love shining in his face. In that past time, the babe was me, and my dear mother was still alive.

"Mia," I say quietly. I scrub the hot tears from my cheeks. Jack steps into me, offering comfort as he places his arm around my waist and emits the low rumbly purr.

"Aye, your mother's name," Pike says, pressing a kiss to her fluffy baby hair. "That is perfect, lass. She is perfect."

He does not yet know that Mia is destined to become an omega. I did not know at first what the strange awareness burrowing in my chest was. But as Molly later explained to me, sometimes a change can occur to a beta mated to an alpha when she bears an omega child. I can now feel my mates' moods, and they mine, like a little thread hooked into my heart.

A gaggle of womenfolk and younger children gather around us and demand their time with the babe, giving my father a moment to compose himself. These same women smile where they once watched me leave with an air of doom, for the eastern clans are well known for their savagery.

I have seen firsthand that savagery. I hope to never see it again. But I have also seen their love, humor, and fearlessness, and their unwavering dedication toward protecting our babe and me. With my two barbarian mates, I have been blessed by the Goddess herself. I only need to look at my sweet little Mia to know I am blessed once again.

The women coo over little Mia. Some remember my mother and comment on both the name and her pretty eyes.

"She will be running around and up to mischief before you know it!" one woman comments with a smile.

I want to keep my little baby girl, but I also want to see the woman she will one day become. I want all the parts in between. There will be times when I scold her. There will be tears, temper tantrums, and naughtiness of all kinds. Likely there will be illness and sorrow as we journey through this life. But there will be joy too, and I will gather all that joy to me, for you never know when the Goddess may call a person to her side.

"She will need a little brother or sister soon," another lady says with a wink.

I smile. Then my eyes shift to the side where Jack and Fen are talking to my father. They are both watching my reaction to the young woman's question with dark hunger in their eyes.

Not only in their eyes. The little thread connecting the three of us pulls tight, coiling all the way to my womb.

They have been patient with me while I learned the ways

of motherhood with little Mia. But I think I am ready to begin again.

"I cannot wait for your tits and belly to grow when you are ripe with child," Jack had said as we bonded inside my father's tiny cottage. *"You will make a good little breeder for my brother and me. You will not want for our attention."*

At the time, his words had seemed barbaric, and arousing for reasons my more innocent mind did not understand. Not once have I wanted for their attention or worried that their eyes might stray elsewhere.

Just as they willingly care, provide, and protect me, I joyously offer them my body and my love, and the Goddess willing, more children.

My smile grows sly. As I look away from my mates, a familiar flutter settles low in my belly. I see a future before me that is beyond all my dreams. I see brothers and sisters for little Mia. I see all the joyous years between now and when one of us must leave this earthly life and join our Goddess. So many years, so many smiles and tears. So much love shared and demonstrated by hot rutting in the furs.

My chest feels full of all the love. I am ready to burst from the joy within me.

Today, and this evening, is the sweetest of moments. Food is brought, and an impromptu gathering takes place.

The sun has sunk low, and lamps have been lit. Little Mia is napping against Fen's shoulder by the time we are ready to take our rest. Papa offers to stay with his old friend Pete, giving the cottage over to us for our use.

"I left the crib out," my father says gruffly. "Happen it might be better placed returning with you for Mia. And any other little ones that might come along."

Tears prick my eyes again as I hug my father goodnight.

"Thank you," I say. "I thought one of my sisters had taken it for sure. But I should love to take it with me for Mia."

"It's not only the crib," my father says, giving me an indecipherable look. He gestures toward my mates as they come to stand with me. "Happen it's time for me to hand over the business to someone younger. An' your older brother is coming to settle here. Jack and Fen suggested as I come an' live with you. My eyes aren't so sharp for some of the more intricate work. But I can still offer some blacksmithing. By your mates' account, the clan is in need of one."

"Oh!" I say, looking to Jack and Fen, who both grin. I guess this was what they were talking about.

"Go on, lass," my father says, looking unusually bashful. "Happen I must be goin' soft in my old age when I've no doubt there'll be more brats on the way. I'll not get a moment's peace!"

He takes his leave, off to join old Pete, and we head inside the cottage.

The quietness inside is strange after the chatting and merriment of seeing old friends. The old crib has been readied and laid out, waiting near to the bedding nook. I smile as I run my fingers over the worn wood. Many generations of my family have slept inside. It will be put to use again for my daughter.

Fen passes the sleeping bundle for me to lay her in. And how wonderful to see her lying where my brothers, sisters, and I have slept. As I look at her sleeping, I see my younger siblings as they were once. Time contracts and stretches, taking me backward and then forward.

The Goddess moves in mysterious ways. As I watch a sweet baby sleeping, I see her work at play.

As I turn from my babe, I draw a ragged breath at the need shining in my mates' faces—Jack, stern, older, and Fen, younger, and sinful in his beauty.

"So, this is where it all started," Fen says with a smirk as he eyes the bedding nook.

"It is a little cramped," Jack says, kicking off his boots and reaching for his belt. "But we will make it work. For we have a sweet little beta mate who needs to be bred."

About the Author

Thanks for reading *Trained for Their Pleasure*. Want to read more? Check out the rest of my *Coveted Prey* series and my other books!
Amazon: https://www.amazon.com/author/lvlane

Where to find me...
Website: https://authorlvlane.com
Blog: https://authorlvlane.wixsite.com/controllers/blog
Facebook: https://www.facebook.com/LVLaneAuthor/
Facebook Page: https://www.facebook.com/LVLaneAuthor/
Facebook reader group: https://www.facebook.com/groups/LVLane/
Twitter: https://twitter.com/AuthorLVLane
Goodreads: https://www.goodreads.com/LVLane

Also by L.V. Lane

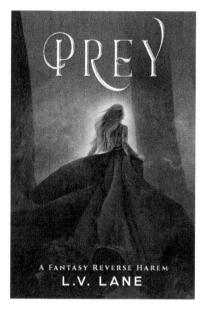

Prey

I am prey.

This is not pity talking, this is an acknowledgment of a fact.

I am small and weak; I am an Omega. I am a prize that men war over.

For a year I have hidden in the distant corner of the Empire.

But I am running out of food, and I am running out of options.

That I must leave soon is not a decision for today, though, but a decision for tomorrow.

Only tomorrow's choices never come.

For tonight brings strangers who remind me that I am prey.

Prey is a fantasy reverse harem Omegaverse with three stern Alphas, an Alpha wolf-shifter, and a stubborn Omega prey.

Printed in Great Britain
by Amazon

42878236R00158